HOLDING ON TO
Nothing

Holding On to Nothing
Copyright © 2023 by Savannah Schmidt

All rights reserved. Printed in the United States of America. No part of this book may be used or reproduced in any manner whatsoever without written permission except in the case of brief quotations embodied in critical articles or reviews. This book is a work of fiction. Names, characters, businesses, organizations, places, events and incidents are either the product of the author's imagination or used fictitiously. Any resemblance to actual persons, living or dead, events, or locales is entirely coincidental.

Contact Information:
https://www.savannahschmidtbooks.com

Front Cover Design by: GetCovers
Editor: Whitney Morsillo

ISBN: 979-8-218-17799-7

First Edition: May 2023
9 8 7 6 5 4 3 2 1

Dedicated to my loving husband.

Thank you for always believing in me.

Now

Connor

I scowl in frustration at the many cars that refuse to drive around the very large puddle of water that forms because of the uneven street, splashing me as they race by. In defeat, I close up my umbrella and stand in the pouring rain, patiently waiting for the pedestrian signal to change. Another car speeds by, and the puddle sprays my face again. "Oh, come on!" I scream, annoyed. "Go around it!"

The rain is not what's bothering me. In fact, on any other day, I would laugh at the situation. It's the fact that I am mentally and physically drained from everything that can possibly be going wrong right now.

The dark clouds clash above and are followed by a flash of light. The city is drowning, and I can't help but think to myself how much of a coincidence it is that it's been raining ever since our accident.

I raise my arm, checking my calculator watch. It beeps, letting me know that another hour has passed. It has been three weeks, two days, and an hour since I last talked to both of them. And it has been three weeks, one day, and twenty hours since the sun has shined.

Lillian and Jasper both suffered traumatic brain injuries, leaving them in a coma, and the doctors tell us all we can do is wait.

Just wait.

They say they can hear you even in the depth of their slumber, but I doubt it. I hope they're dreaming of somewhere nice and warm. Somewhere safe and wrapped in each other's arms.

I only walked away with a few bumps, but a lifetime of trauma. Trauma from the never-forgetful event. I was the only one to get through it all, and I have to watch the world live on while they lay there. Motionless. It honestly angers me. Why am I not lying in a bed somewhere too?

It seemed to happen all so quickly. Like ripping off a bandage from a freshly cut wound. There's no way that Jasper could have seen the truck coming. It came out of nowhere, then all at once, knocking us off the side of the road.

The light finally changes, and I am welcome to cross the street, to continue my journey to the hospital. That's all I've been doing for the past few weeks. Every day, I trek through the pouring rain, hiking across town to see them. I'm tired and might as well live here because I don't want to be anywhere else.

I cross the parking lot and scuffle my feet through the front doors, the cold air conditioning embracing me. The smell of lemon fresh cleaner fills my nose, followed by a hint of coffee from the cafeteria. The lobby is kept occupied by strangers and the patients' family members.

I wince in embarrassment as my shoes begin to squeak across the tile floor, leaving wet footprints behind. I reassure myself that I'm not the only one and continue on my way past the front desk and down a long hallway to the elevators.

The hospital staff is kind enough, I think. They take great care of my friends and Jasper's mother, who refuses to leave her son's side. They also have become accustomed to seeing me every morning before I go to work.

Once on their floor, I make my way toward Lillian's door first. I knew Lillian just enough, but not enough to sit and have a conversation with her in her sleep. I still find it odd but want to be respectful and say hi. She would kill me if she knew that I didn't.

I wave to the usual staff members and pass the nurse's station. My shoes come to a quick halt, screeching loudly against the freshly polished floor as I hear my name being called down the hall. "Hey, Connor!"

I twirl in place, the head nurse standing in the doorway of another patient room. She leans against the doorframe with a smile on her face and a clipboard in her hands. "Lillian is on a different floor," she gushes. "She's awake! She woke up last night."

I feel as if my lungs are deflating. The air escapes as I gasp silently to myself. "D-do you know what room?"

She shakes her head. "Check with the front desk. And congratulations, Connor!"

I sprint back down the hallway to the elevators and press the button a thousand times, impatiently waiting for the doors to burst open. Excitement radiates through me, escaping through dancing feet. I eagerly watch the numbers descend until it dings at my floor.

I ride the elevator back down to the ground floor, sprinting to the front doors. I ignore the line of people who are patiently waiting, sliding in next to an elderly woman who holds herself up against the counter. "Lillian Abernathy," I huff, breathless.

"There's a line, you know," the elderly woman snaps.

"Lillian Abernathy, please."

The woman behind the desk blows a bubble out of her mouth. It pops, and she quickly chews it again. Her eyes squint, and she sighs. "You should know where her room is by now, Mr. Harris."

My cheeks flame. I may have asked the front desk lady too many questions about too many locations. I figured it was her job, but I knew I had gotten underneath her skin. "They moved her to another room."

"I was here first!" the elderly woman scoffs. "Go back to the end of the line!"

"I *really* don't care, lady. This is important."

The woman throws her nose into the air, turning her head quickly away. She stands there quietly. Her fragile hand tightly grips her cane.

"If it makes you go away faster…" The woman behind the counter scowls at me, her eyes lowering back to the computer screen. Her fingertips type away. "Second floor. Room 239."

I crow like a rooster and slap the counter excitedly. "Thank you!"

The elderly woman covers her ears, "Ay yi yi. Maldito desperdicio de espacio".

I grin nervously, not knowing what she is saying, and apologize before sprinting through the halls to the elevator once again. Once on her floor, I gain composure and find myself walking slowly.

Suddenly, I'm nervous. Not a single thought comes to my mind as I attempt to think of things to say. I pictured this moment for the past few weeks, but as selfish as it is, I've been picturing what I would say to Jasper. Then, in a sense, we would be there together when Lillian woke.

As I turn the corner, my eyes beam for her room. A loud, deep voice comes from within, unrecognizable but almost calming. "Alright, Lillian, we are going to ask you a few questions to get your mind thinking. Is that okay?"

"Okay," her voice cracks.

Before I can enter the door, her father steps out. His hands are in his pockets, and a stern look crosses on his face. "Connor," he nods. "I could hear your shoes from down the hallway. Is the weather that bad outside?"

"Yes, sir. There are flash flood warnings in our area for the next few hours."

His eyes quickly scan my body. "I wasn't expecting to see you so soon." James Abernathy was an evil snake that held onto judgement. We were all beneath him, and he only had eyes for shiny riches. He didn't even try to hide the fact that he wanted nothing to do with your presence.

"Why didn't you call me when she woke up?"

He grins. "I didn't want to bother you. It was the middle of the—"

Bullshit. "Bother me? Sir, she's one of my best friends. Do you know how happy it made me to hear that she was no longer upstairs?"

"Yeah, well—"

Before he can finish his sentence, the doctor calls him back into the room, and I'm close behind. Once through the door, the air falls still and the whole world stops. My eyes sting from the tears emerging from deep within.

She is okay. She is awake and okay.

The look on her face says it all. She's scared. She stays silent and listens to the doctor as he whispers to her father. Clinging on to every word, I can almost hear her heartbeat out of her chest.

Mr. Abernathy gasps. "Memory loss? What are you saying?"

My head darts in their direction.

"She remembers certain things, but for right now, everything is still a little foggy. It's normal. Sometimes those memories take time to piece back together, but other times they never recover."

"Never recover?" I blurt.

"I'm sitting right here, you know?" she speaks, her voice slightly raspy. I bet her throat is dry and numb from everything they've been doing to her. "Please don't leave me out of any conversations."

Her father sighs. He reaches up and itches the top of his head, then brushes his hair back. He's a handsome man, I suppose. Or at least the ladies think so. Sharp chin, freshly shaved, and smells like a damn pine forest. He always has his gray hair combed over and gelled slightly, mint on his breath. "Honey, what's the last thing that you remember?"

His voice makes me want to vomit. This silly baby voice he is using, it's not him. It's an act.

Her mind seems tired, but her eyes are wide awake. The way her face softens, searching for answers, you can tell she's trying. Her blue eyes blink a few times as if she's shuffling between memories and dreams. "The last thing I remember is leaving the house for homecoming. Brad and I were on our way to a diner," she explains. She tucks a few strands of red hair behind her ears before sitting up. "Where is Brad? Is he okay? Did we get into a car accident?"

My heart sinks. This was someone no longer in her life. She was no longer in high school and hasn't seen Brad since. It's been at least two years since then.

"Uh, sweetie. He's fine. Don't worry about Brad."

I make my way around the bed and sit next to her. It scares me to ask the millions of questions that swirl in my head, but I have to be certain. *Maybe a few words can trigger a memory?*

"Do you know who I am, Lil?" I ask.

She sucks in her bottom lip and chews on it. "A nurse? A doctor in training? My therapist?"

"Erm, no. Do you know who Jasper is?"

She shakes her head. "I'm sorry, no. Should I know who that is?"

My throat feels swollen, slowly closing, and it's becoming harder to breathe. Tears form in my eyes as I look at the woman who no longer knows who the love of her life is.

The doctor places his clipboard on the edge of her bed, grabs a chair, and rolls it between his legs. He plops down onto the moving stool. "Who is Jasper, son?" he asks, turning to me.

"Is this really necessary? She doesn't need to be overwhelmed with information that she can't even remember," James says, dismissing the question.

The doctor holds up his hand, stopping James from becoming irrational with any further opinions. "I am only seeing how far back her memory goes. I need to make a diagnosis."

7

My eyes shift to Lillian. She stares and waits patiently for me to answer. "Jasper is her boyfriend. The one who she was in an accident with."

The doctor nods and then clears his throat. "Alright, now, who is this Brad fellow?"

"An old flame," James answers. His lips curl into a shit-eating grin. "From around two years ago. Maybe even longer."

My jaw stiffens.

The doctor runs a hand through his dark mess of curls. He sighs and then drops his hand to his knee, slapping it slightly. The look on his face screams bad news. "Retrograde amnesia."

Lillian's father huffs in annoyance, crossing his arms against his chest and pressing his back against the wall. "English, doc. What does that mean?"

"It means that any new information, right before the accident, is gone. She can remember things from years ago, but she can't recall anything up until this point."

Disappointment sinks in. She doesn't know any of us. We are just strangers to her.

I quickly turn away from her gaze and pull myself away from the bed, hurrying into the hallway before the river runs down my face. Throwing myself against the wall, I slide my back down against it and sit on the cold tile floor. I cover my face with my hands and cry.

"Connor," her father's voice becomes clear. "It'll take time for her memories to return, but she will remember."

I pull my hands away from my face and peer up at him. He tries his best to have composure, but he holds a smug look. I rip myself from the floor and find my feet. "And if they don't? She forgets all the memories we made over the last few years and forgets who Jasper is. I know you never liked Jasper, but whether you like it or not, he is a big part of your daughter's life."

"I know, I know. But maybe this is best for her. She can return to her old life and finally move back home. She needs her family, Connor. I don't know what Jasper put into her head, but I am glad it's gone. She nearly ruined her life."

Anger boils beneath my skin. He never understood his daughter and tried his best to control her. She finally broke away from it and developed happiness in her life. She felt like she was living her own life and not someone else's. It took her a while to break all the habits that she grew up knowing, but she was finally free in the end.

"You ruined her life," I nearly scream. "That's why she never wanted to have a relationship with you. She wanted to do her own thing, and you kept her on a leash. You treated her like a polished trophy. You never asked her what she wanted out of life and never once asked if she was happy doing the things you wanted her to do. She was happy with us."

His lips slightly part as shock runs through his body. His green eyes squint at me. "If Jasper was the love of her life, where is he now? Why isn't he here to defend himself? Oh, wait, he can't. He's the one who put her in that damn bed. He is the one who put you all in danger in that ever-loving accident. How is that love, Connor?"

Lillian always spoke highly of her father, even if she had mixed feelings about him. She understood the science behind his ways, but I never did. Jasper tried, but he couldn't wrap his head around it, either. Deep down, she always had guilt built up inside of her. She hated the way things turned out and often wished he was different, but she knew her father would never agree with the life she lived. She was just accepting the truth before the accident, ready to close that chapter of her life, but things have a funny way of unraveling themselves.

I can't believe this. Lillian... our Lillian doesn't remember a damn thing. She is back under her father's control and in purgatory.

"You fucking hypocrite," I spit. "What do you know about love?"

Before James can reply, a nurse stomps around the corner. Her ponytail swings back and forth behind her. "Hey! Do I need to call security? We don't tolerate this kind of behavior in the hospital. Take it outside!"

I couldn't stay and argue with Mr. Abernathy anyway. I knew we couldn't agree on anything, and it would be a continuous cycle. We both had opinions on Lillian's life and what we both thought would be best for her at this moment, but we were both in the wrong. It wasn't up to us.

"No," I calmly said. "I'll leave."

❈ ❈ ❈

My head falls against the glass window, my breath fogging my view. He lies in bed, stiff. They tilted his sharp chin back. An air tube is down his throat, and wires are connected to every part of his body. His chest rises and falls slowly.

It kills me to be the only one who remembers the accident. To be the only one who walked away with a few scratches and bruises. It could have been a lot worse. It should have been a lot worse.

A hand touches my shoulder, and I am pulled back into reality, a shock running through my body. My heart races as a gasp escapes my lips. I spin my head around and find myself smiling. "Mrs. Smith."

"Sorry, I didn't mean to scare you." She lightly smiles. Her doe-like eyes are tired. Dark circles form beneath them. She pulls her dark hair into a messy bun.

I watch as she makes herself comfortable. Anna sets her purse down beside the empty recliner chair and pulls a sweater over her bare shoulders. She walks over to her son and brushes his dark hair away from his forehead. She bends down to kiss his cheek, whispers she loves him, and then strokes his hand before peering back at me.

I join her at her side and watch as his chest rises and falls. His skin is pale and fragile, and a few scratches stretch across his cheeks. His eyelids are a shade of blue.

My heart aches to see my best friend like this, but I know he will wake up soon.

"How is she?" Jasper's mother asks.

I nod. "She's okay. She's awake, but she has no memory of anything that's happened."

"That might be a good thing. The accident was terrible."

"I meant like no memory at all. She can't remember the last two years of her life. She doesn't know who we are."

Her eyes roll to the back of her head, and she scoffs. "I bet her father is loving that."

I shove my hands into my pockets. "Oh, you know it. We have already exchanged words."

"Poor Lillian. I can never understand why parents love the control over their children. Let your children be happy, or they will resent you for the rest of their lives."

I reach up and scratch the back of my head. I'm at a loss for words but completely agree. "I just don't know what to do about the situation. I doubt he will let me see Lillian now," I say. "It was a different story when she was asleep."

"Hopefully, she gains back her memory. Jasper will be heartbroken when he wakes up to learn she can't remember him. He won't know what to do without her."

"Him and I both," I sigh.

I lean my back against the wall, casting a shadow over his body as the sunlight beams through the window. My head cocks to the side as I watch his machine count his heartbeats. "I need to speak to her again," I continue. "Alone."

"Just sneak into her room. You have every right to see her as they do."

"What about the staff?"

"Make up some bullshit lies. Connor, I know damn well you and Jasper used to lie to my face all the time in high school."

I break into a smile. The shit that we used to do, I'm surprised we didn't kill each other back then.

Now

Lillian

The room is quiet. They've finally left me alone with my thoughts and feelings.

I enjoyed the company of my father... I think. It was nice to have familiar faces greet me when I woke up yesterday, but I despised it soon after.

My father is still the same, even in a crisis. He treats me like an object and not his daughter. I don't think, no matter the circumstances, he would have changed. He will still be the same. It humors me to watch him change in front of people. To pretend to be a whole different person.

But for right now, I am alone and so very thankful for the silence.

Father had some kind of meeting and promised to be back later. He also promised to bring back some egg drop soup, my favorite. By the time he comes back, he will complain about how busy he was and how he had forgotten about dinner. So, I'll offer room service, and he will act like the hospital food is beneath him.

The boy's face pops into my mind as I lay here with my hands at my sides. I knew him. I must have. The look on his face said it all. The confrontation outside the room just confirmed it.

I questioned my father's motives. He's hiding something from me, but he wouldn't dare speak the truth.

That's why he turned that boy away. It just made me more curious and determined.

I use my hands to push myself up in bed, propping myself up against the stiff pillows. The IV pulls at my skin as it pumps medicine into my body. The hospital bed isn't comfortable, the room is cold, and my back is hurting.

The hospital staff is fairly nice, though. They monitor my machines and often refill my water pitcher. I can't do anything for myself at the moment, but I hate having to ask for things.

Growing bored, I look around the room for any of my things. No purse or phone in sight. I couldn't learn about myself, even if I tried. I'm positive Father made sure of that.

I think about watching television, but the man down the hall would ruin that. For the past hour, he screams or talks loudly to anyone who walks by his room. I don't want to be another bother if I turn the television volume up to drown out his voice.

Shifting my view toward the door, a pair of shoes squeaking against the tile. I see blue eyes looking around the corner and into my room, his body hidden.

The boy—Connor.

"He's gone," I nod. "You can come in."

His dirty blond, shaggy hair bounces as he enters the doorway, his freckles scattering on the pale skin of his cheeks. He smiles and quickly shuts the door, holding a book underneath his arm. "Hi," he nervously says. "I, erm, I hope you don't mind me shutting the door. I just needed to see you, and I know that I'm not allowed to be in here."

"Not allowed to be in here? Why?"

He clears his throat and quickly takes off his jacket, hanging it over the back of the guest chair. He pulls it closer to the side of the bed and sits down, laying the book on his lap. "I know you from the two years that are missing from your brain," he explains. "He was never in the picture in the last two years, and he thinks seeing me will bring back those memories."

My head spins. *I finally got away from him, but how?*

"That's amazing," I breathe. "I've always wanted to be on my own. I wanted my own life and my own experiences. I want to make mistakes and learn from them. I don't want a safety net."

His lengthy body moves the chair closer. He takes my hand, and weirdly, it feels familiar. The warmth seeps into my skin.

"I know. Your life is so amazing, Lillian. You are a stepmother and a best friend, and you found a love for antiques. We go scavenging for them on the weekends usually."

"Wait, what?" I cut him off. "A stepmother?"

"Well, I mean, not yet. You will be soon. He was going to ask you to marry him."

"Who was?"

"Jasper."

I swallow hard and try my best to picture this life. A life that was finally mine. I couldn't imagine it, though, no matter how hard I tried.

I was going to get married and be a mother to a child that wasn't mine?

"What happened to going to school for my law degree? I applied to Stanford University weeks ago. Did I get in? Did

I at least graduate high school?" I look down at his hand holding mine. "What about Brad? What happened to him? What happened between us? Did we ever get married? When did we break up? Was he angry? I bet he was angry."

He squeezes my hand. "Lil, calm down."

My head spins. From the pain, trauma, and everything in between, I'm confused, angry, and helpless. "Calm down? My whole life is a mess! I have a life I don't even remember, and I have so many questions, but no one seems to have the answers or wants to give me the answers."

He slightly laughs, holding up his book. "I have all the answers you seek," he says, trying to sound mysterious. "I went home last night and wrote down everything I remember from the past two years. Maybe this will trigger some memories. And if not, you got to hear an amazing story about how my two best friends fell in love."

"Forgive me, but how could you possibly know anything about my life and how we fell in love?"

He grins. "Jasper. He's my best friend. We tell each other everything. He told me everything and anything about you. Almost as if he was trying to process the information himself. He could go on and on about you."

I take a deep breath and swallow hard. I feel nervous learning about a life that I have never lived, or at least, in my mind I haven't. Coming to terms with it, I get comfortable. "This is going to be super cheesy, isn't it?"

He shrugs. "Maybe. But isn't every love story?"

"Love," I snort. "I haven't been in love with something since my rabbit died."

He shakes his head as his fingertips tap on the cover of the book. "Putting everything else aside for the moment, how are you feeling?"

That's the one question I wished people would ask more. Instead, they look at me like a scared, fragile child. So, they treat me like one.

I'm not a child anymore. I'm an adult now. I'm eighteen.
But I'm not. I'm not eighteen anymore.
I'm twenty.
I am twenty years old.

My chest rises and falls. "I hurt. I'm weak and tired," I say, as I clear my throat. My eyes search the room as my mind races. "I'm twenty years old, Connor. I know age is just a number, but I don't feel twenty."

My mind is panicking, and I can't control it.

He studies my face and soaks my words up. His smile is wiped away from his face, and he stands. "Why don't you get some rest, hm?"

I reach for his hand. "Please don't go. I didn't mean to scare you. I just haven't had a moment to myself since I woke up, and I'm still trying to process everything."

He squeezes my hand. "You didn't scare me. It just made me realize that I should give you space. I don't want to suffocate you. I know you're already getting enough attention from your father," he jokes, a small smile creeping upon his lips.

There is something sweet and kind that he holds within his voice. Just by his demeanor, he is nothing like my father. Nor a prodigy of his creation.

"Please stay," I beg, as I look up at him. His blue eyes are soft. "I don't want to be alone. I could use a friend right now. I need a distraction."

He nods and sits back down. He pulls on the bottom of the chair and scoots it closer to my bedside. He leans back and opens the book. "Okay, but if it gets to be too much, just tell me to stop, and we will stop. Okay?"

"Okay."

Then

Lillian

Sometimes I wish my mother was alive *instead of you. It sickens me to know how perfectly you try to present yourself on the outside, but in reality, you are hiding something dark on the inside. It's hard to watch you be a leadership figure for everyone else except for your only child. Blood is all you will ever see us as. I'm just a label to you.*

You set my whole life up. Ensured I'm enrolled in a private school, involved in some sort of school activity, and have the perfect boyfriend. All to make me happy, right?

You set me up with another version of you. It makes me want to hurl. And I try my best to put effort into this so-called relationship, but it just doesn't seem right. It's forced and awkward.

Mother wouldn't agree with any of your actions. She would want me to be taken care of but loved. Mother would be proud of you for becoming mayor of our little shitty town. She would allow me to have freedom in my life, no control. Mother would allow me to make mistakes, even if they made you look bad. She loved me.

As for you, you're downstairs drilling my boyfriend about his future in football.

Laughter fills the air and grows louder as it slips beneath the crack at the bottom of my door. It crawls beneath my skin and sends a shiver down my back, a sigh escaping from my lips.

"Lillian," my father calls. "Don't keep this young man waiting!"

I bite on my bottom lip and stare at my reflection. I'm a senior, an adult at eighteen. I decide on a black slim attire for my last year. Last year, I had the whole ball gown, princess getup, but I'm not that girl anymore. The more I try, the more I've come to realize that I can't make my father proud. He always demands more.

I curl my dark auburn hair and primp my eyelashes. Then, I apply dark eyeliner around my bright blue eyes and paint a few more layers of makeup on, darkening my red lipstick with black. For now, I like this view. *Your reaction will be well worth it.*

"Lillian," he calls again, in a deeper tone.

I roll my eyes in annoyance. I grab my purse and jacket from my bed, taking one more glance in the mirror before heading out the door. My heels click against the hardwood floor.

I hear my father cuss under his breath and climb the stairs. "Lil—"

I meet him at the top of the stairs. "If you call for me again, like one of your little rat dogs, I will scream."

Speechless, he moves to the side to let me by and follows me down the stairs. I feel his eyes evaluating my attire, but he doesn't dare say a word. I know it makes his blood boil because I don't look like a classic barbie doll.

I lightly smile at Brad as he holds out his hand to help me down the rest of the stairs. His dark eyes follow my every move, and a smile perfectly crosses his dimpled face. I wonder if this is a scene or if he actually thinks that I'm pretty.

It isn't Brad's fault he was raised a certain way. Like myself, his family expects the world from him. He's the son of a wealthy and crooked judge, his mother a stay-at-home wife. They're hard on Brad, and his father often leaves evidence of that. We were just puppets in our parents' little show.

"Gorgeous," Brad admires. His black bowtie is tightly hugging his neck, making his body very stiff. He's handsome and belongs on the cover of a magazine, but I know he'll end up bald and fat in the next thirty years.

My father scoffs.

"Thank you," I nod. "You don't look too bad yourself."

My father passes by us, his hand reaching for the door. "Would it kill you to lose the dark lipstick? You look fucking ridiculous," he whispers under his breath. "You are going to homecoming for Christ's sake. That dress is too revealing. Cover yourself up."

There it is. I knew he couldn't keep it inside. He can act this way around Brad, but he wouldn't say anything like this in public. It would ruin him.

Brad, giving me an apologetic look, takes the small black jacket from my arm and drapes it over my shoulders. He kisses my cheek. "Ready to go? I hope you're hungry. The boys are waiting for us at the restaurant."

My father holds the door open with his foot while he digs into his pocket for his wallet. He hands Brad a few hundred-dollar bills. "Get her another dress. Something that won't show cleavage and isn't funeral themed please. She is so depressing to look at."

Before Brad can comprehend what my father is asking, I rip the money from his hands and stuff it back into his coat pocket. I narrow my eyes at him. As my cheeks flush, I feel a hot sensation, and my eyes begin to burn. "I don't understand how you can stand there and say that to your only daughter," I say, as my voice cracks.

"No daughter of mine will dress like a whore," he argues back. He shoves his hand back into his pocket and slaps the money into Brad's hand. "Get her out of here. I'll see you later."

The ride to the restaurant is quiet. I am aggravated and tired of fighting with my father. It's a daily battle, and I often stay locked away, hiding in my bedroom because of it.

I pick my head up from the window and peel away my jacket from my shoulders. I flip the visor down and wipe the tears from my eyes, making sure my makeup doesn't smear. After digging into my purse, I apply my lipstick. "I'm sorry you had to see that."

"I'm used to it. Our fathers are the same. It's ironic, really."

I laugh, pushing the visor back up. "Please keep the money. I don't need another dress. He won't even notice," I say. "He acts like I don't even exist at home anyway."

"At least your father ignores you. Mine hovers over anything I do and corrects me if I'm doing anything wrong."

The car grows silent again.

His eyes shift to me. "You shouldn't drive your father crazy like that, though. You know how he will react to things, so try to avoid confrontation. Kiss ass."

The lump in my throat grows. His attempt to have a decent conversation with me slightly surprises me. I almost feel like he's even trying to coddle me, but I should have known better. He couldn't be sensitive for one second without bringing the asshole side of him out.

"Kiss ass? All we do is kiss ass! Our whole lives have been kissing and literally up their asses because they want us to be fucking silver spoon babies. I'm tired of it."

"What's wrong with that? They pay for everything, and we get to ride through life without problems."

I raise an eyebrow. "You can't be serious. They lay our whole fucking lives out for us, and you don't see a problem with that?"

"No? Why should I? I mean, I hate my dad. But I'm also grateful for the things he has given me and for the things he plans to do for me. He just wants me to have a successful future."

I don't reply. It's pointless because we don't see eye to eye on anything. He likes the life that was planned out for him. That's the difference between us and our shitty lives.

I clear my throat, sit up straight, and put a fake smile on my face as the restaurant comes into view. A few of his friends stand outside, waiting for our arrival. They get rowdy as Brad's car pulls into the parking lot.

I feel a burning sensation in my chest as I get angry again. It doesn't surprise me in the slightest because Brad can never have a second alone without his friends. It was challenging to try to form a genuine connection with him. We've been in a relationship for almost two years now. We're both virgins and refuse to show any public affection for one another. The worst thing we do is probably hold hands.

"Brad, my dude, you look awesome! Where did you get the tux?" one shouts, as he opens the driver's door.

"My old man. Fits like a glove," Brad chuckles, as he steps out of the car. The door slams behind him, and I watch as his friends follow him down the sidewalk. They laugh and slap each other on the back as they enter the restaurant, leaving me alone in the car.

I bite my lip and throw my head back against the leather seat. I can't believe this is my life, and I so badly want it to change. Graduation can't come quickly enough. I'm grateful to be going soon and to be able to change my life without my father being involved.

I watch as Brad's tall body comes out from the small restaurant, rushing to my side and opening the passenger door. He rests an elbow on the top and leans in. "Why are you just sitting here? I thought you would have followed us in. You're embarrassing me."

I scoff. "Embarrassing you? I'm the one embarrassed. I can't believe we call this a fucking relationship. It's an arranged engagement. There's no love or even friendship. It's forced and fucking disgusting."

He sighs, "I'm trying, Lillian. It's been two years, and I'm trying to make this work for the both of us so we aren't at each other's throats."

"It's honestly sad. We don't even act like a couple. You act like my chaperone more than anything. We haven't even kissed!"

His large hand runs through his short, dark hair. It's perfectly gelled in the front to push off of his pale forehead, his caramel eyes searching mine. His sharp jaw clinches, and

I can tell that I made him think. His hand reaches down and wraps around my small chin, his thumb rubbing my cheek.

"Do you want to be kissed, Lil? Because, dammit, ever since I met you, I have wanted to kiss you. I have wanted to touch every inch of you, but I have been so damn scared of you."

"Scared of me?"

"You're so damn mean. So bitter to me. It's okay to not like the life we live right now, but I promise you that everything that I plan to do is for you."

"You never talk about us," I hiss, as I pushed away his hand. "You're teasing me. You don't care about me. Our parents tell you to, so you think you do. I like how you just flip a switch and force yourself to say some bullshit like that to me."

Then

Lillian

You can't blame this all on me, Lillian. I know you don't have feelings for me. If you did, you'd make the first move."

"You're right. I don't have feelings for you because we never built that connection. We haven't learned anything about one another besides the obvious issues with our parents."

His lips snake into a smile. "That's okay. We can learn about each other for the next eighty years."

I place my heels on the pavement and rise out of the car. "Yeah, if we don't kill each other first. But you're right. You are stuck with me until the very end." I force a smile.

Rolling my eyes, I spin around to close the door and find myself off balance as an arm wraps around my waist. His breath is heavy against my ear as his lips brush my skin. "You want more passion? I'll give you more passion, Lillian. I hear your wants and your needs. Just say it."

"That's not what I meant," I huff. "You know that."

With his hands placed on my hips, he spins me back around and pushes me against his car. He's handsome, but he feels like a stranger. I've known this guy all my life, but this is someone different. He's acting. I tell myself this over and over—it's an act. He's such a two-faced piece of shit, and it's draining.

He brushes a strand of hair behind my ear and kisses my forehead. A sigh of relief escapes my lips. I wasn't ready for our first kiss, especially one that was threatened.

"I promise to try, but only if you do. Otherwise, we are wasting our time, and your father will not be getting any more money." He narrows his eyes at me. "You don't want to ruin his life and reputation, do you?"

I bite my lip and think about how much I could affect his life. I'm certain that Brad's family has a tremendous secret that would make my father's life hell. Brad wouldn't hesitate to go to his parents if I jeopardized it. That's the price to pay for living in a small town full of families that go way back.

I nod in agreement for now, but I have other plans. I often think about trying to convince my father to move away with me, but I don't see that happening.

"Good, girl. Now kiss me," he says, as he leans in. He forces his cold and sloppy lips onto mine, attempting to deepen it.

I feel like I'm drowning and pull away. "Let's go inside. I'm starving."

❀ ❀ ❀

Ordering food for myself has become a huge ordeal lately, and apparently, I can't be trusted. I eat rabbit food at least twice a day except for breakfast. Weekends are a free for all, but I crave something other than just lettuce. There's only so much you can do with the damn thing. I want meat. Nothing plain or dry. Something greasy and juicy. Meat that is bound to give me heartburn later, maybe even clog an artery or two.

Sometimes I sneak off in the middle of the night to grab a cheeseburger, but not as often as I would like to. Father won't let me eat anything greasy. He says it will make me fat and give me a "pizza face." That's the last thing I need to do is give my father more reasons to yell at me.

So, I try to get away with it today.

I attempt to order a cheeseburger, but Brad quickly turns it down, ordering a house salad for me before ripping the menu from my hands and giving it to the waitress. "You know the rule, doll. You can't have that garbage," he says. "It's not good for you."

His friend laughs. "What? She can't order for herself? Why can't she have a damn cheeseburger?"

I reposition my body and turn toward Brad. I place a stern look on my face and wait for his response. "Yeah, Brad. Why?" I mock.

He shoots me a glare. "She has health issues." He then pushes the question away quickly, changing the subject. "What did you guys think of Saturday's game? Wicked, right?"

Smooth. Real smooth. Asshole.

After a while, I feel like my mind is ready to explode. I'm losing brain cells by the second hearing the four of them talk. I'm not surprised by their mannerisms or their colorful vocabulary, but I expected more out of them when it comes to being in public.

I've only hung out with the guys a few handfuls of times. Mostly at house parties or town gatherings. This is my first time spending time with them alone.

I watch as the blond-haired guy devours his second cheeseburger. The ketchup smears across his cheeks as his lettuce and tomato slip out from beneath his bun and onto his plate, his fingers quickly scooping them up and dumping them into his mouth. His blue eyes dart over, and he grins, sticking his tongue out. He shows me his chewed-up food and laughs.

I suck my bottom lip in an attempt to not throw up. I glance down at my plate and begin to pick at my salad. I'm starving, but not for this trash.

"Lillian, you haven't said one word to any of us. That's kind of rude," the blond snickers.

"It's hard joining in on a conversation that I know nothing about," I say, as I pick up my napkin from my lap. I dab the corners of my mouth and watch as all eyes are on me.

Brad's hand reaches below the table and pats my knee. "You would think you'd know more by now. Football is probably the only thing I ever talk about."

It's honestly one of the biggest reasons why I ignore you all the time, I think.

Biting my lip, I poke my salad with my fork and sigh. My stomach growls, and my eyes grow wide as a pile of fries just sits on Brad's plate. He hasn't touched any of his food because he refuses to shut up. Golden fries with steam still rising through the air.

Take one, my inner voice screams. *Just one. What's the worst that can happen? No one is even looking, Lillian. They are busy with their conversations. Just. Do. It.*

My hand slowly rises, and my eyes shift between the plate and his face. My fingers wrap themselves around a crinkle fry, the cut potato burning my skin. I wince at the pain but quickly shove it in my mouth. My mouth opens slightly as I let the air cool my mouth down, the French fry burning the roof of my mouth with every chew.

His lips stop moving as his face darts in my direction. I expect him to yell at me. Or even hold my lips shut so the French fry can melt the skin off the inside of my mouth for stealing it off his plate.

Instead, he surprises me by saying, "Would you like another? I'm not that hungry." He scoots the plate closer, knocking my salad out of the way, then proceeds to join in conversation with his friends, placing his hand back on my knee.

After nearly eating all the fries, I wipe my salty fingers onto a napkin and ball it up into my fist before placing it back on the table. For once, I feel happy and satisfied with my time. I didn't engage in their weird conversations, but I did what I wanted. And for once, he let me.

"Do you know if Destiny is coming to homecoming, Lillian?"

"Dude, you should have asked her to homecoming!" another guy says.

"He's chickenshit," the blond-haired boy says. "He won't even ask her for her number. Let alone fucking follow her on Instagram."

The curly-haired brunette cowers in the corner of the booth. His cheeks turn a shade of pink, and he grows quiet. He was the only respectful person in the group.

"I just—"

"Just. Just. Just," the blond kid mocks. "Just what? Fucking spit it out, Romeo."

Brad's domineer changes. "Enough, Sam. Leave Jason alone."

Sam smiles mischievously. He quickly wraps his arm around Jason's neck and pulls him into his chest. His hand quickly reaches up to ruffle through Jason's mop of curls.

"Aw, come on, Brad. He knows I'm only fucking with him. Someone has to push him out of his shell. How else is he ever going to get any pussy? He needs to get his dick wet before college."

"Really?" the last one says, as he drops his burger from his mouth, the sandwich landing on his plate. "Is that all you ever think about?"

"What?"

"Pussy."

"Well, William, when you put it like that—"

"Enough," Brad interrupts. "Can we just have a normal conversation without bringing up provocative stuff? Please?"

"Please," William groans. "We get enough of this shit in the locker room."

Sam lets Jason go, sighing. "Fine. Fine," he mutters.

Jason pulls his phone out, looking at himself in his camera to fix his hair.

Brad sighs and looks down at me. "Are you doing okay?"

Before I can answer, Sam clears his throat, loosens his tie, and begins to play with his food.

"Oh, Brad?"

He pulls away from me. "What, Sam?"

"Fuck. You."

As the words spill out of his mouth, his hand tightly grips what is left of his cheeseburger. The food was mushing between his fingers. He pulls his arm back and throws it forward, the food landing on Brad's chest. Ketchup smears onto Brad's white long-sleeve button-up shirt. The food falls onto his lap, and he lets out a loud growl.

"What the hell, Sam?"

"Fuck. You," he repeats.

"You're fucking dead," Brad threatens.

Laughter pours out of all the boys' mouths as they all begin to throw food at each other. They eventually rise to their feet and continue to smash food into each other's faces.

Milkshake splatters against Brad's chest. The sweet and sticky substance trickles onto my face. I wince, a gasp leaving my lips.

Embarrassment and anger pour over me as people stare. The servers whisper to each other behind the counter, and the dinner settles into stillness. Everyone watches the boys and doesn't say a word.

Why would they? They know their parents. They know the hell they would raise if they spoke to them. Cowards.

"Boys," I say. Not loud enough, though, as they continue. "Boys!"

They stop. Food drips off of their faces and onto the floor.

"Everyone, shut up! The queen has something to say," Sam smirks. Mashed potatoes are smeared across his forehead, and mustard is on his cheeks.

"What are you doing? You are acting like fucking children. Grow up! We are practically adults now. Act like it."

Jason and William sit back down. They stare at the mess they've made and begin to pick it up, raking the mess off the table and onto their plates. "Sorry," they both mutter, ashamed of their actions.

"Don't tell me sorry," my voice grows louder. "Tell everyone in here sorry. They are the ones who have to pick this shit up and deal with stupid ass people like you."

"Hey!" Sam barks. He slams his hands onto the table and leans forward. "You don't get to speak to us that way. I don't give a shit who your daddy is or who your mama used to be. Without Brad, you would be a nobody. Got that, princess? You'd be someone in the shadows, hiding behind every crowd. Your daddy? Well shit, he would be working in a dump like this. Or worse. Probably even dead. So, be grateful. Brad could drop you in a hot minute. He can have anyone. He doesn't have to be with you. Brad can easily make some shit up. Tell his dad some lie about how you spread your legs for anyone in town. You maybe even gave him some type of disease. Who the hell knows? Point is—learn your place. Two years, Lillian. You should know it by now."

I bite my lip, looking up at Brad. "Are you going to get your mutt?"

He blinks at me and sits down. "No," he replies. "He's right."

I half laugh. "So, everything we spoke about outside, that all just went right out the door. Didn't it?"

He stays silent.

I shift my body toward him. "And you want an honest relationship? To hell with that," I murmur, sliding out of the booth and walking out of the diner.

Now

Connor

By now, I am sitting next to her on the bed, and our shoulders are touching. She leans over and grabs a box of tissues, drying her eyes. When she looks back at me, her cheeks are flushed, and her blue eyes are bright. Her eyes are glossed over and red.

"What's wrong? Are you remembering?" I ask. My voice was full of hope and concern.

Am I hurting her by telling her the truth? Is it my place to be doing this? She deserves the truth.

She shakes her head. "No." She sniffles. "I just... this is terrible."

"I know my handwriting is awful," I joke, nudging her with my elbow.

She cracks a smile, laying her head on my shoulder. "No, my life. It's terrible.

"I'm sorry, but no. This was your life before Jasper."

She becomes silent. A few tears roll down her cheek as all these thoughts and memories soak into her. "I always knew my life was hell, but hearing it from someone else's point of view, it's sad. Like why didn't anyone else notice it?" she questions. "Has it always been this way?"

Her father's abuse wasn't obvious. He let his words be his weapons of mass destruction. Her father loved the thought of his words becoming eternal wounds for the soul. He felt accomplished that way.

And sadly, this was the aftermath. He lost everything and everyone because he chose wealth and power over his daughter, who ruined him. Ruined his reputation and the life he lived. He was now the outcast of the town, and he hated it.

"Well," I say, "you've been in this lifestyle for so long that you couldn't notice it. It was normal for you. You didn't see it until you broke free."

"My mind can't wrap itself around this. It's disturbing and disgusting. It wasn't just how I was treated but also how I acted. I woke up and felt different, but my mind remained the same. I feel misplaced. And my mind still holds my escape plans and all of my hatred."

"How about we take a break?" I close the book, but her hand grabs mine and stops me.

She shakes her head. "Please don't. I'm enjoying the story. Oddly enough. I just want to remember. I want to remember the perfect memories and not the bad ones."

"Your story is a mixture of both. It's okay, though. We can only see rainbows after we endured the storm." I smile lightly as I open the book back up. "Or whatever weird people say to make themselves feel better."

She rolls her eyes. "Alright, quit distracting me. We are about to get to the best part."

Before I can continue with the story, we are quickly interrupted. We both become silent as the door slowly opens. Her father walks into the room with Brad not too far behind.

Mr. Abernathy grows amused by my presence as if this was a race. How quickly could I save Lillian again before he snatches her up and takes her away for good? He likes this game. Too much.

"Oh, hello, Connor. It's nice to see you again," he nods. "You remember Brad, don't you?"

Sweat trickles down my back. I knew he had a plan up his sleeve.

Brad pushes past Mr. Abernathy and comes to Lillian's side, sitting on the edge of her bed. He takes her hand and brings it to his lips and kisses it.

Kissing her hand *repeatedly*.

When I see them together, I feel sick to my stomach. She has him and their relationship etched deep in her mind. Jasper is nowhere in sight. Erased. Gone.

"How are you, Lil?" His other hand reaches for her face, and he softly brushes it with his thumb. "I've missed you so much."

She laughs slightly. "To me, no time has passed by."

His head falls as he laughs. When he lifts his head back up, tears form in his eyes. "Lillian, the world is such a scary place without you. I didn't know what to do. You left me broken," he say. "You hurt me so bad."

I swallow hard as anger swallows my pride. I can't listen to any more of this bullshit.

She just woke up, you piece of shit. Why are you making her feel bad for something she doesn't remember? It's not all about you. But you take every opportunity to make it about yourself. Don't ya?

I keep my thoughts to myself and decide to leave the room. I swing my legs off the bed and onto the floor, setting the book down on the chair. As I leave the room, her father leans to the side and places a hand on my shoulder to stop me. He snickers to himself and brings his lips close to my ear. "Don't think I didn't know you were in here. The nurses called me as soon as you stepped foot onto the floor."

I pull away from him. "And?"

"I'll allow you to see her. Let you fill her head with pointless stories and junk, but she's still coming home with me. And she's still not going to gain her memories back."

I turn to look back at her. Lillian almost looks happy, but hesitant. She doesn't want to go back to her old life, but she finds comfort in it right now. She finds comfort in him.

I could never amount to that. No matter how much I desperately want to, I won't.

❀ ❀ ❀

Jasper's chest rises and falls slowly.

I watch the monitor as the green line goes up and down, creating squiggles across the screen. His heart rate counts up and then counts back down, changing periodically. The machine that feeds him through a tube beeps.

"Oh! I'll go get the nurse. I think it's time to change his food bag," Anna states, as she pushes herself up from her chair. "I'll be right back."

Once she has left the room, I take her seat next to Jasper and grab his cold hand. "Hi there, buddy. How are you? We miss you." I sigh and hang my head. "Jasper, life would be so simple if you were awake. This shit is ridiculous. I don't know how you put up with Mr. Abernathy for as long as you did. And Lillian…" I continue. "I don't know what the hell to do. You are so much better at these things than I am. You know me, I'm just a giant fuck up."

I push back the hostile tone in my voice and take a deep breath.

"Sorry. I talked to your son this morning. He's so worried about you. I tell him all we can do is pray about it and be positive. It's not much of a positive situation, though, is it?"

I begin to tap my foot, my knee bouncing as I grow anxious and sweaty. "Lillian lost her damn mind, and you are asleep. I can't help my best friends, and it drives me fucking insane. What am I supposed to do, Jasper? Tell me. I am suffocating here, bud."

"Connor, honey, you can't solve everyone's problems. The world just doesn't work like that," Anna says from the doorway.

I drop Jasper's hand and rise to my feet abruptly. My eyes are wide as they land upon her silhouette. "Mrs. Smith, I'm so sorry."

"You're okay," she shakes her head. "Do you know how many times Jasper has had to lie there and listen to my rambling? Poor thing can't talk back or walk away from my obsessive talking."

I chuckle. "I just needed to vent. Even in a deep slumber, he is still a good listener."

She half laughs and enters the room, standing at the end of his bed and staring at him. "You sound like me. This whole situation pisses me off. I'm grateful for everything the doctors are doing, but there has to be more they can do. I miss my baby."

"I know. It's difficult. You're doing all you can do."

"So are you. You're doing more than enough. You don't realize how much help you have been. Between checking in on my grandson, telling Lillian stories, and visiting Jasper… then on top of it, you are going to work in the afternoons to keep the bills paid and food on the table. You are doing amazing. Thank you."

"Jasper would do the same thing for me if I were in his position."

Then

Lillian

Where are you going, Lil?" Brad calls from behind me.

I hear the diner's glass door slam from behind me, the bell inside clashing against the glass.

"Away from here! I'm fed up with this bullshit."

My heels click against the pavement as I walk to the edge of the parking lot. I stand at the edge of the road, my arms crossed against my chest. My cheeks feel flushed. I'm so angry I could cry.

"Lillian," his voice is closer now. "Get away from the road." "Why?" I spin to meet his gaze. "I can hike my leg up, show some skin, and try to hitch a ride? Maybe even offer my body to a kind stranger in exchange." I shrug. "Because, ya know, that's just the type of girl I am. A girl who sucks dick for a living to pay my daddy's bills."

"Will you calm down?"

"Calm down?" I scream. "You want me to calm down? You hypocritical bastard! Quit filling my head up with bullshit, and I just might be alright."

"I'm sorry."

Thunder rolls in, the sky growing dark as rain pours. The hot pavement lets off steam.

"Come on. Let's go inside and talk," Brad says, as he grabs my hand, attempting to yell over the sound of the rain.

I yank my hand away from him. My hair sticks to my bare skin, my makeup smearing as the raindrops flow down my cheeks. The cool water feels good against my heated skin. "Do you want to know what the sad part is? I was actually starting to like you. You were gaining my trust slowly. And I was excited about tonight's dance. But like everything else, you ruined it."

Stains cover his outfit from food still left on him. The smell of the mashed up food poisons the surrounding air. "I can make it up to you, I swear. Let's just go back inside," he begs.

I want to believe him. I want to keep making this work, but I know it won't change. "No," I growl. "It's too embarrassing. You let a bunch of airheads boost up your ego. It's embarrassing to be seen with you when you act like a bunch of fucking cavemen."

"Embarrassed to be seen with me?" he chuckles. "That's rich."

"You can't drop something. Can you? You always have to have the last word."

"Will you just shut up, Lil? You have one active and wild imagination. Do you know that? Quit overthinking things, and get inside the damn diner. I said I'm sorry. Lillian, I can change. I'm trying to change for you."

I shake my head in disbelief. "You wouldn't treat me the way the you do if I was Rileigh," I mumble.

He rolls his eyes and points a finger in my face. "Don't you dare say her fucking name! Leave her out of this. She's gone now, thanks to you."

I laugh, throwing my hands up into the air. "The truth comes out! That's why you hate me so much! You blame me for everything that happened."

"I didn't say that."

"You didn't have to! But I have news for you, Brad. It's not my fault. I didn't agree with this stupid arrangement, either. Blame our fucking parents. To think this was ever going to work. To think you can just throw together two people and expect them to fall in love. It doesn't work like that."

His face falls. His anger lifted. That's all he was, just angry. It wasn't my fault, and he has to realize that. "Do you want the truth? Why I'm so incapable of loving you?"

I blink at him. My chest rises and falls, attempting to catch my breath. My jaw relaxes. "Go for it. Please, be my guest."

"I was so in love with her, Lillian. I planned to marry her when we graduated from high school. She was my first everything."

"And where is she now?"

"I don't know! Ask my father."

"Why? Because he didn't want you to be with her?"

"At first, he didn't mind it. He liked her. He didn't mind her family, either. But then I got her pregnant, and he thought my whole world was over."

"And then what happened?"

He runs a hand through his hair and cries, "He made her get an abortion. Paid her parents off and made her leave. He told me that he didn't want me to breed with someone like that. Trash, he called her. He wanted it to be you. It was always you."

My heart shatters. I finally got to the root of his problem. Why he's never touched me in two years and why he's never treated me like an actual girlfriend. He doesn't want me. He wants her. Brad doesn't love me. He loves her.

42

I shake my head. "What's so special about my family, then? Why does he want me?"

He shrugs. "I always thought it was about money, but then I learned that he is paying your father. So, now, I don't know."

This town is crooked and dark. The original families go way back, and they stick together. They keep this town up and running, happy and sheltered from their business behind closed doors. The rain lifts, and the sun peeks through the dark clouds.

I clench my toes, uncomfortable in my shoes. The material is now wet, and my skin raw, creating blisters. I step out of one and reach down to grab the other, holding both by the heels. My toes stretch out against the warm, wet pavement.

His friends come out one by one, shoving each other and laughing. They slide onto the front of Brad's vehicle and start hollering. I can only imagine the damage they did after we left.

He turns to look at them. "Erm, don't tell the guys about that. Alright? They know he made her leave, but not the complete story."

I nod, motioning to my lips being locked and the key being thrown over my shoulder.

"Go take care of them. Take them home with you and hose them down." I give him a small smile. "You all need a shower."

"Do you want me to take you home?"

"No, I think I just want to be alone."

"Lil, your father—"

My eyes turned a shade of red as the anger inside of me just wants to burst out. It's as if my water bucket is full, and with every drop, it threatens to overflow. I'm tired of my life being controlled. I just want to have a simple thought for myself.

I laugh. "I swear to God, Brad. If you say something stupid about my father, I will jump off a bridge head first."

His mouth parts. "I didn't mean to upset you."

"Just please give me this one day. I know we both have our issues going on right now, but I would love nothing more than to be alone." I sigh, looking away from him. "I appreciate you telling me everything that has been bothering you lately. I appreciate you for wanting to fix things between us, but for right now... Please, just leave me alone. I just need to think."

He nods and doesn't say a single word.

I watch as he makes his way back to his car. One of them climb into the vehicle with him and the others get in the vehicle they arrived in. Both cars pull out of the parking lot and leave, honking on their way down the road.

I'm alone.

Finally alone.

The cool breeze flows through the autumn trees, making goosebumps rise upon my pale skin, my body damp. Cicadas sing from the trees and grass, screeching their song.

My head turns to look at the diner. I feel ashamed. Deep down, I know I should go back inside and help clean up, but I can't face it.

My thumb anxiously rubs against the leather strap of my purse as it hangs off my shoulder. It dangles at my side and I itch for... something.

Anything.

I've never been left alone before. Usually, it's just at home and in my room. But never in public. I'm always surrounded by someone and doing something.

My head cocks to the side, catching sight of an old red Coca-Cola bottle machine that sits across the way against an old barn that was once transformed into a mechanic shop. The machine is rusting, but I hear a buzzing noise faintly coming from it.

Curiosity draws me to the machine.

My grandfather always loved soda out of a glass bottle. He swore it was better that way than out of a can or plastic bottle. He promised to get me one but passed before he could ever do so. I was eight years old then and forgot about that memory. Father made sure of it. Erasing anything fun in the world.

Not today. Today, I'm doing what I want.

Looking back and forth, I skip across the street and onto the dirt road. My feet sink into the wet dirt, the warm mud oozing between my toes. I smile, wiggling my toes around.

I can't remember the last time I placed my foot on the grass or dirt. Father doesn't allow it. He says that the only grass or dirt that is allowed on clothing is from the golf club or a beach resort. I wasn't allowed to get dirty growing up. It isn't proper, and it isn't ladylike.

I raise my head to look at the old machine, determined to take a sip from the glass bottle. Even if the soda was old and disgusting, I still want to say that I did it.

I dig out coins from my purse, my body inching closer to the machine. I put the change into the machine and carefully listen to it tick. It moves the glass bottle and eventually drops it.

I lean over to grab it, the glass nice and cold. I pop the cap off with the side of the machine; the soda bubbling over. I laugh and quickly bring it to my lips as I slurp the bubbles away. Titling my head back, I take a large gulp.

The bubbly substance is flavorful as it goes down my throat. It's fresh and not at all how it usually tastes. Cold and carbonated and yummy.

"Oh my gosh," I gush, looking at the bottle.

"That good, hm?"

I jump, holding the bottle by the neck and bringing it into my chest.

The dark voice comes from inside the barn. A large body comes out of the darkness and into the sunlight, a face matching the voice. He wipes his messy hands on a rag and then wipes his brow. Black oil smears across his forehead.

His blue eyes smile as he stares at me. He licks his lips and shakes his head. "Sorry, I didn't mean to startle you."

"Sorry, I didn't know that this place was still up and running."

He chuckles, looking up at the old wooden building. It leans to the side but still has every board intact. The big white sign is a shade of brown now, but once said *Tony and Son's Shop* in red ink. "She's a little dirty and a little old, but yeah, we are still keeping her alive."

I lower my guard, relaxing my shoulders as I sip on the soda again.

He continues, pointing to the machine. "It's been a while since I've had anyone come and bring more of those, so I don't know how old they are."

"It's still enjoyable. It doesn't taste old at all."

"Good. Good," he nods. His eyes rake the ground. He bites his lip as he thinks about what he would like to say next, but stays silent.

I roll my eyes. "Spit it out. I'm not going to bite."

Then

Lillian

Are you sure? Because that argument with your boyfriend looked intense to me. You looked mighty angry," he says, his country accent thick. "Don't take offense at the things that I say. It was hard not to overhear your conversation... even in the rain."

"He isn't my boyfriend," I snap, as I take another sip from the bottle. "And stay out of my business."

"Everyone in North Georgia was in your business, darlin'."

I glare at him, taking another sip from my drink. I think after a moment of silence. He looks familiar, but I can't pinpoint where I've seen him before. "Do I know you?"

He pushes his black hair away from his forehead. "I doubt it, but I know you."

I snort. "Everyone does. That's what's wrong with this town. Everyone can't help but be up each other's asses. I doubt they would want it any other way. Everyone is so nosey."

"Or just the higher families are. Everyone knows those who have a little lick of wealth, but when it comes to less than anyone else, they don't pay attention. Unless something extreme happens. Then it becomes a juicy topic for you people."

"I don't have time for this," I dismiss him. I shake my head, turning away.

Is he trying to start an argument? I think. *He doesn't know me. He just knows of me.*

"Lillian," he says. He leans to the side so our eyes meet. "I'm picking on you. It's Jasper. Jasper Smith. You don't remember me?"

I shake my head. "Should I remember you?"

His shoulders slump, and he looks around. "Really?"

"Really! Now, are you going to stand there and make me guess, or are you going to tell me where I've seen you from?"

His eyes grow wide, but he grins, showing dimples in his cheeks. He has my attention, and he's liking every second.

"High school. I was two years ahead. I was on the football team with Brad and Jason." He pauses for a minute, then blushes before adding, "I asked you to prom?"

I frown and shrug.

"Damn. It kills me you don't remember me. I had a huge crush on you."

My fingers clench tighter around the heels of my stilettos, my teeth digging into my bottom lip. I honestly tried my best to remember, but can't. "I'm sorry," I say. "That was, what? Two, three years ago?"

He nods. "About three, I'd say. But that's okay. I dropped out a year later, my senior year, because I ended up having a son."

A light bulb goes off inside of my head. I faintly remember... "You were dating that horse-looking girl, weren't you?"

His face falls, twisting into disgust as his brows narrow. "Her name was Skylar," he corrects me. "But yes, I ended up getting together with her."

I look down at my muddy feet. My toes wiggle as I grew nervous. I didn't mean to make him upset, but that's just how everyone identified her. "How is she?" I want to be nice and have a conversation, but the truth is I already know what happened to her. It was the biggest talk in the town. High school dropouts have a baby, and the mother dies during childbirth.

"She died giving birth to our son."

"Oh, I'm so sorry—"

He raises a hand. "Save it, Lil. I can't take any more of your fake behavior." He turns on the heel of his boot and walks back into the barn. Dirt covers the back of his white t-shirt, his jeans tight around his butt.

Those jeans.

"It was nice seeing you, though," he adds over his shoulder.

"Fake? You think I'm fake?"

"And shallow and ignorant," his voice carries, as he disappears inside.

I follow him. "You got that all in the two seconds I've been standing here?"

"Pretty much. You're not the Lillian I remember."

He gets back onto the ground and climbs beneath an old red truck, his legs squirming as he attempts to fix something underneath the vehicle. He grunts and groans, "Dammit."

"People change, ya know."

"No, they changed you, and you let them."

Deep down, I know he's right, but I refuse to allow him to know that.

He fumbles through his bag of tools, the metal clinking together as his hand rummages through them. He grabs what he needs, and his hand slithers back underneath the truck. "Mother fucker," he mumbles, as he tinkers.

"Well," I huff. "Tonight, I'm doing what I want. I refuse to go to homecoming, and I stood up to my father for the first time... so that counts for something? Right?"

He sighs. "Yeah, sure."

"Yeah. I'm not sure what Brad and I are, honestly."

He drops his tool onto the ground and climbs out from underneath that truck. He dusts his hands off on his jeans. "Why are you telling me all of this bullshit?"

"Well, I just thought—"

"Oh, you just thought that since someone gave you a little lick of attention you would just tell your entire life story, is that it, huh? I've got news for you, darlin'. We aren't pals. You can save it for someone else because, in those last two seconds of talking to you, you lost all my respect."

"What? How?"

"Oh, I don't know. Maybe talking shit about my dead girlfriend?" he snaps. His face falls in embarrassment, and he quickly covers his face. "My mama would kill me if she knew I just talked to a woman like that. I apologize."

The pressure lifts off my shoulders, and the feeling of almost having to put my guard up stresses me. I always have my guard up around Brad, but that's because he's unpredictable.

"No, I'm sorry. I shouldn't have said that. It was disrespectful and wrong. I just don't know my limits and have no filter." I shrug, leaning back on the truck. "I don't put anyone's feelings into consideration. I only think about myself."

He climbs to his feet. "There she is. That's the Lillian I used to enjoy being around.

"You're going to have to refresh my memory because I still don't remember ever hanging out together. So, I don't know what Lillian you are referring to."

"Oh, I have some stories." He takes the glass bottle from my hand and points to my dirty feet. "But, if you are sticking around for a while, we are going to need to get you some shoes and not the ones in your hands." He narrows his eyes. "How the hell do you even wear those things? They are like five inches tall."

I look down at my toes and wiggle them. My yellow fingernail polish shines through the now crusted, dry mud stuck to my skin. "What's the matter? Don't like my toes? I didn't bring anything else. I was supposed to go to homecoming, remember?"

He throws the almost empty bottle in a large metal garbage can and disappears into a doorway off to the side. He comes back, clicking his tongue against the roof of his mouth and carrying an old pair of boots in one hand. With his other hand, he loosely carries a beer by the neck of the bottle.

"Here," he says, as he throws the boots. They tumble in the dirt and eventually land at my feet. "There are too many nails and old shit lying around here. I don't want to see you getting hurt." He pops the cap off of the bottle and sips it, watching as I bend down to grab the old leather boots. He motions to the back of the barn. "There's a hose in the back to wash off your feet. If you keep that mud on you, you might catch a ringworm or something gross."

"Thank you."

I drop my heels and purse to the ground, then push them against the truck's tire with my bare foot, hugging the dirty boots against my body. Normally, I would freak out about my dress and my shoes getting dirty, but not today. I'm not going to let my brain think. I want to be as normal as I can be, even if that means getting dirt underneath my manicure.

I tiptoe around him and cautiously make my way to the back of the barn, slipping through the crack between the large barn doors. The grass is overgrown in the back, but the view from the bottom of the valley is priceless. Rolling hills for miles, gradually growing larger and turning into dark blue mountains.

The crickets hum a song, a warning sound for all as I walk through the tall grass. I make my way to the side and turn on the silver spigot. Cold water falls and turns into a small stream, flowing down the hill and disappearing into the grass.

I squeal as I rinse my dirty legs and feet off. My eyes glance into the distance as the sun disappears behind the mountains, turning the sky a reddish pink. The clouds trail off into the sky, and stars appear faintly.

"Would it be wrong of me to offer you a beer? You're eighteen, right? That's close enough."

His voice trails off as he peeks outside, watching as I struggle to put the boots on. With both of my hands on the barn, I balance myself and place each foot in its place. Oddly, they fit.

"Those are my mamas," he nods. "She hasn't worn them in years."

"Why not?" I squeeze myself between the crack of the doors again and meet his gaze, taking the beer from his hand.

"She used to wear them every time she came to spend time with my daddy in the shop. When my daddy died, she had no reason to come down here anymore."

Jasper motions for the beer back, grabbing the neck. He digs into his pocket and pulls out his keys, taking an old copper one and jamming it underneath the cap of my beer bottle. He pops the cap off and hands it back to me.

I follow him back to the front of the barn, my boots scuffling on the dirt floor. I carefully maneuver around the old red Chevrolet pickup truck, watching my step.

He slides back into the side room, this time turning on the light. The lightbulb swings side to side as he grabs the tiny wooden stool from underneath the desk, picking it up with one hand and pulling on the string to turn off the light with the other. He plops the stool down against the wooden wall and then grabs his beer from the truck's hood and takes a seat on the ground, his back resting against his truck tire.

"It changed her, didn't it?" I sit on the small stool, my knees tightly kept together as my dress rides higher up my thigh.

"Slightly," he answers. "If anything, she shut those pieces of her life out. She's gotten a lot better, though. She's not as depressed anymore and is starting to come back around. I think having my son around helps her a lot. Keeps her mind off things."

"What about you?"

"What about me?" He slightly chuckles, taking a sip from his bottle. "Did it change me? Fuck yeah, it did. My daddy was the greatest man alive. He taught me everything I know about working on vehicles. He taught me how to be a noble father and the traditions I plan to pass down to my son. After my daddy's funeral, I came to the shop and sat in the office at his desk and cried. Eventually, I found peace and began to pick up where he left off." Staring down at the beer in his hands, he sighs. "He died a year after my son was born. It was a tough two years. Losing the woman I loved and then my father. But my mama and I got through it. Together."

I smile sadly. "He'd be proud of you, Jasper."

"I'd like to believe so."

❀ ❀ ❀

Drinking through his six-pack of beer, we talked for hours underneath the dim lights of the barn. My bottom became uncomfortable against the hard wooden stool, so I join him on the ground. With my legs stretched out and crossed at the ankles, I lean my back against the wall.

"Wh-what time is it?" I ask, drunk.

"Way past my bedtime," he groans, leaning to the side and pulling out his phone. The screen is cracked. "Midnight."

"Mm." I lean forward and snatch the phone from his hands. My thumb runs over the cracks in the glass. "You need a new phone."

He chuckles. "Oh, you think? I mean, it's a great phone. I can't text or call anyone, but I can answer phone calls."

I wiped my lips off after guzzling the last of my beer. "How am I supposed to give you my number if your phone doesn't work?"

His smile disappears, and his cheeks darken to a shade of red. "You want to give me your number?"

I scoff. "Yeah, why not? We had a great night. Or at least, I have."

"I haven't had a reason to use my phone in a while. I have only one friend, and I don't really call him. He just shows up whenever he wants to, plus I work with him half the time. I take calls from the office phone for services or appointments."

I hand him his phone, the screen lighting up midway, revealing a picture of his girlfriend and son. He sees the sadness in my eyes and stuffs the phone into his pocket. Almost as if he's embarrassed.

I lightly smile, setting my bottle down and climbing to my feet. Stumbling to the wall, I catch myself from falling. "My father will send the sheriff looking for me again if I don't get home soon."

"Again?" His grin grows bigger. "I'd love to hear that story."

"That is for another time. I have to leave some mystery to keep you thinking of me."

"Oh?"

"Yup."

He climbs to his feet. "Let's get you home, you flirt."

My head feels fuzzy and light, but I feel free. At this moment, I don't want to stress myself about my life, even though I know that I don't have the right mindset. I've been enjoying myself and the company that I've been with.

"You're driving? But you had more beer than me!"

"Darlin', I've been drinking almost every day of my life ever since the love of my life died. I could drink a whole keg by myself and not feel the littlest bit tipsy." He picks up all of our empty bottles and throws them away in the trash can. "Let me turn all the lights off and lock up the shop. I'll meet you outside."

I lean over and scoop my heels up by the straps, flinging them over my shoulder, and wobble outside. He pulls down the garage door behind me and locks it into place, with a few more doors and locks following it.

I kick at a rock and look across the empty road. The diner is left in the dark without a soul in sight. I'm sad about my experience there but enjoyed the fries at least.

The cool autumn air nips at my skin as my hair whips around in the wind. The moon hangs bright in the night sky, and the stars twinkle above, the night full of the sounds of the weeds and trees brushing against each other, fireflies blinking in the distance.

I don't want to go home. I don't want to go back to my life. If I could live outside without a care in the world, I would.

The sound of gravel crunches underneath tires from behind me, the truck quickly coming to a halt. The brakes moan in a gut wrenching squeal. "Are you ready?"

"No, but I have no choice, right?" I spin on my heel and lock eyes with him as he leans over the steering wheel of his truck. The passenger window is down, his face almost dissolving into the darkness. "Where were you hiding this thing anyway?"

57

"On the other side of the shop. I usually park over there and leave the front for customers," he says, as he opens the door for me from the inside. The interior lights turn on, and the darkness fades away. His blue eyes are now dark and nonexistent in the night. "It's this or my motorcycle."

Something inside of me explodes. "Motorcycle? You chose this over a motorcycle!"

I climb into his Ford and slam the door, my skin pressing up against the cold leather seats. My teeth are chattering, and I shiver, dropping my heels onto the floorboard and quickly buckling up.

"Maybe next time I'll give you a ride on that, but for right now, you're too drunk. It's too dangerous, and I don't want you getting hurt."

I stick my tongue out and then let out a long yawn. My eyes feel heavy. "You're no fun."

❀ ❀ ❀

After explaining to him where I live, it isn't long before I make myself comfortable. My eyes become heavy, and eventually, I fall asleep. He turns on the heater and melts away all of my shivers. The radio silently plays in the background.

"Hey, I think we're here."

It's hard to pry my eyes open. I fell asleep hard and fast, time escaping me. I sit up and squint my eyes at the monstrous tower that I live in. The porch lights are on, but the house is dark.

My mother chose every detail of the house. It hasn't changed, and it never will change. It'll still be a giant white house with black shutters. She had planted red roses circling the large dark porch, little lights hidden here and there to light up the walkway at night.

I squint my eyes at a little flashing light in the window. The living room television is on, and instantly, I feel the need to puke.

I groan, "Mother flicker."

"Excuse me?"

I quickly turn to look at Jasper. His face is pale and reflects the lights from the porch. You can almost see the blue hidden in his eyes.

"My father," I say. "He's awake. He must be waiting for me."

"What a good daddy," Jasper jokes, laughing slightly.

I scoff, opening the door and hopping down onto the pavement. I lean in to grab my heels, dropping them at my feet, and kick off the boots. "Thank you again, for everything." I slide them to the floorboards. "It was nice to have a day for myself. To do what I wanted."

"Of course. I'll have to steal your number from you so we can do it again."

My mouth drops. "Shit. I forgot my purse at your shop."

He grins, turning his head and leaning back. He reaches for something in the back seat and then throws it into the passenger seat. "I found it while locking up. It was stuffed under my daddy's truck," he mocks me.

I rip the purse off the leather seat and close the door. "Funny. You're really funny." I blink rapidly as my body sways. I lean against the door of the fancy truck, digging through my purse for my phone. "What's your number, Jasper?"

The bright screen nearly blinds me. I whine from the pain and headache that it causes me, stuffing my phone back into my purse. I quickly cover my face and rub my eyes. "Never mind. I'll just call the shop later to get it," I mutter.

"Good, because you owe me a story."

"And you owe me a motorcycle ride."

"It's a date then," he chimes.

"A date?"

"A date."

I hold my head. "Remind me about it tomorrow. I might not remember."

"Alright, will do, darlin'. Now, get inside and go to bed. Don't forget to drink water and take some ibuprofen before bed."

I snort, "darlin'."

He rolls his eyes. "Inside now, Miss Abernathy."

I salute him. "Yes, sir!" I push myself away from the truck, shuffling my feet across the warm pavement to the porch. Feeling as if my feet were stone, I climb every step to the front door and begin digging in my purse for the keys. The keys jingle in my hand, and my tired eyes grow heavy.

I look up and wave to Jasper, expecting him to leave, but he doesn't. Instead, he waves back and continues to wait. His mother raised him to be a gentleman.

Just as I'm about to put the key in the door handle, the door opens. My father towers over me. "Where have you been?"

"What?" I stumble over my own two feet as I push past him and into the hallway. "I've been with Brad."

My eyes glance at his television show, but I quickly feel sick. My stomach turns, and my throat tightens, my forehead sweating. I throw my shoes down and make my way to the corner plant, picking up the large pot and throwing up all over the fern.

The door slams. "That's nice. Really nice. You're drunk."

I put the plant back in its spot and wipe my lips off with the back of my hand. A sour and distasteful flavor is left in my mouth. "It's okay. The puke acts like a fertilizer and gives nutrients to the plant," I giggle. "So, in a way, you are welcome."

"That's not cute, Lillian. Not in the slightest."

"Your dogs puke all the time. How is that any better?"

"Because they aren't drunk when they do it! They are dogs with stomach issues!"

Even in the dark, I can see the scowl on his face. His hair is a mess, and he's in his robe, his glasses pressed against his face. He never stays up this late.

He sighs and rubs his fingers over his eyebrows. "Just go to bed. I don't have time for this. I have meetings in the morning. I'll call Brad's parents tomorrow."

"What? Why?"

"Because that behavior is unacceptable. It's not going to happen to you."

"How do you expect me to ever live a normal life if you don't let me live at all?"

"You can live a normal life, but there are rules."

"Rules? That's all my life is! You keep me locked away and only let me come out when it's beneficial to you. I'm talking about a life where I am allowed to have fun and do what I want to do. Where I make mistakes and learn from them. Not because you told me it was a mistake."

He stays silent for a moment before saying, "I'm going to get onto Brad for not buying you another dress, too."

I scream and brush past him, stomping upstairs.

"I'm your father, Lillian. There are rules for a reason. You can't just do what you want. The town will judge you for your mistakes." He follows me up the stairs and turns on the hall light.

"The town can go fuck themselves. They aren't innocent, and neither are you. I don't understand why everyone tries to be so perfect. We don't live a perfect life." I stop at my bedroom door, hearing his footsteps not far behind.

"Language," he warns.

I turn to face him. "That's all you got from what I just said?" I challenge, squinting my eyes at him.

"No, I'm listening."

"Are you? Because how many times have I told you that I hate cheerleading? How many times have I told you that I don't want to go to college to be a lawyer?"

He stays silent.

"You are so busy trying to make sure I make you happy by doing the things you want me to do, but you don't even care for my happiness. What kind of father are you?"

Then
Lillian

Everything I do is for you, Lillian, to make sure you are taken care of and to have a successful future."

"Yeah… yeah… yeah. I hear ya, sperm donor."

He squints his eyes at me, his bushy dark eyebrows lowering. "I don't understand why we have to fight about it. What is this game that we are playing?"

"You tell me! Because I don't understand why you are so far up Brad's parents' asses. So, you tell me what game we are playing. What's so special about them, huh? Why do they pay you money and give you what you want? We didn't come from wealth, so I don't understand what makes you so valuable."

"Forget it. Get some rest." He turns away and walks back down the hall.

"No, tell me. What makes you so special? What are you hiding from me?"

"Drop it," he yells, stopping at the edge of the stairs. "It's none of your goddamn business."

I bite my lip, and my eyes cower.

He turns the light off and heads back downstairs, the television volume increasing. Applause is heard, and laughter is behind it. He loves watching game shows, but lately, he hasn't had time to watch them.

In another world, my mother would be here instead of you. In another world, we would live perfectly as one. A perfect little family, but the image only lives in my mind.

I turn my doorknob and enter, closing the door behind me. I drop my purse to the ground and toss my shoes at my closet door. My brain pounds against my skull, pressure emerging from behind my eyes. I'm tired and ready for bed.

I'm thankful that tonight was mine. I could only imagine what homecoming would have been like if we would have attended. Brad would ignore me for more than half of the night, then ask me to dance when the DJ calls for the last song. He probably would have won homecoming king and would be forced to take pictures. He would have enjoyed the night because this is the only time he will ever peak in his life, and then we would have attended an after-party. I would sit in the corner and listen to gossip from the girls on my cheerleading squad, get drunk, get hit on a few times, and then beg Brad to take me home.

I was content with my night and couldn't care less what Brad did with his.

I unzip my dress and clumsily find my way to the shower, dropping my bra and underwear at my feet. I bend down and turn the faucet on, the hot water blasting out of the shower head. The steam swirls into the cold air, the mirror fogging up. I climb into the tub and pull the curtain closed, sitting down. I let the water fall like rain, massaging my back as I hug my knees and lean forward.

Is it strange that I just spent the entire night with a stranger? Then, I let him get me drunk. Is that normal? Tears prick at my eyes before a small smile crests my face. *Everyone is a stranger in the beginning,* I think. *It's fine. He didn't kill you. You just made a new friend. A normal friend. A friend that is yours and only yours. It wasn't forced, and it wasn't imaginary.*

After the shower, I pull on a tank top and some pajama shorts, then pull my wet hair into a messy bun and climb into bed. The cold sheets felt good against my soft skin, my body sinking deeper into the mattress as I lay there.

Staring at the ceiling, I smile to myself as I think about the time my mother let me have the leftover Christmas lights to decorate my room. I never took them down. The white lights continue to dangle from the ceiling. That was five years ago.

My phone buzzes on the side table, and I quickly turn over to retrieve it.

What the hell, Lillian? What did you do? Brad texts.
What do you mean? I replied.

Your father just called my mother. He's beginning to suspect that we know that something is going on.

Because something is going on! I questioned him when I got home. He was quick to shut down the subject. Something doesn't seem right, Brad. Why are your parents so interested in a man who comes from Minnesota? I text back.

Does it matter?

Yes, it matters. Don't you want to be free? Otherwise, you are stuck with me.

It's not all that bad, is it?

It could be worse, I guess, but I don't think we see eye to eye on things. Maybe I just don't like being told what to do, otherwise, it wouldn't be such a terrible life. Right?

He sends another text. *All I'm saying is I want this to work. This thing between us.*

Really?

Yes, so please stop trying to ruin my life and go to bed.

I don't reply. Instead, I plug my phone in and roll over. I pull the covers above my shoulders and bury myself in the warmth of my blanket.

I don't care what Brad has to say about it. I want to know the truth.

❀ ❀ ❀

A week later, I find my father passed out at the dining room table one morning, a bottle of wine in his hand. His mouth is slightly open, drool dripping from his lips as he snores against the wooden surface. He usually could keep his composure, but lately, not so much.

I guess I was to blame.

I sigh, roping my tie around my neck and placing it perfectly in the front. They force us to wear such attire. I understand it's a private school, but is it really necessary to have uniforms?

They force girls to wear plaid skirts with white button-down tops and a tie wrapped around their necks. It's the same attire for boys, but instead of skirts, they have to wear jeans or khakis. People still add their own little style to the outfit, but nothing too noticeable.

"Quit fucking watching me. Don't you have somewhere to be?" he groans, as he lifts his head from the table, "Get lost, kid."

"Aspirin is in the cabinet next to the sink," I say, leaving the room and stepping into the hall. I grab my keys from the hook next to the front door and wonder if I should take his keys, too. Leaving the house is the last thing he needs to do. "Stay home today."

"Don't tell me what to do, Lillian. I'm not a child," he yells from the kitchen. He digs through all the cabinets, cursing under his breath as he slams one and opens another. "I have a meeting today."

"When? Because it's almost nine o'clock."

"You're lying," he growls.

"Nope," I yell. I rock back and forth on my feet, staring at the ceiling as I listen and wait for his response.

"Christ." He rushes around the corner and hikes upstairs. "Why didn't you wake me sooner?"

"You didn't ask me to?" When he disappears, I spin around and take his keys. "Tell your bimbo assistant to drive you to work today!"

"What?" I hear faintly.

"Nothing. Bye!"

I quickly stuff his keys into my purse and head straight for my car. Technically, it isn't mine, but once my mother passed away, I didn't dare let my father sell it. It still holds everything she once had in it, almost in the exact spots she left them. A necklace my grandmother gave to her still hangs around the rearview mirror, and a few cardigans are stuffed in the back seat. She had gone shopping that morning and died that evening, the shopping bags still full and in the trunk. The seats still hold her perfume and the radio still plays her Shania Twain CD.

My mother had to have an old classic car. Not just any classic car, but a yellow Volkswagen Beetle. It was cute.

I swing my bookbag off of my shoulder and set it in the passenger seat, then slip my purse strap off my shoulder and fling it into the vehicle as well. After sliding in, I close the door behind me.

I'm not ready for the day, not just because I have a football game I have to attend later, but because Brad asked me to dinner after the game at his parent's house. I can only imagine what they have to say. Especially if it's about my speculations.

This past week, Brad won't acknowledge my questions. He doesn't want to question why our parents are the way they are. He just wants to obey his father and wished I would, too.

I know he's asked me to drop the subject, but I can't. I can't just relax and pretend to ignore everything. Maybe there is a genuine reason, but my father acts too suspicious about the subject. He should have known I would ask sooner or later. I'm not a little girl anymore.

Halfway down the road, my car starts smoking and makes gurgling sounds as I pull over to the side, my chest tightening from the anxiety. That's the last thing I need to hear from my father. Another reason to get rid of my mother's car.

"Shit," I curse, as I hit the steering wheel. My forehead falls against the leather of the wheel, and I shake my head. "I know I didn't want to go to school today, but I needed a better reason than this. Not my mother's car!"

Luckily, I haven't made it into town yet, and we live off the outskirts of it. I can't have someone find me, and word get back to my father, not yet anyway. Leaning over, I grab my purse and begin rummaging through it to find my phone. I quickly scroll through my contacts and call Jasper. I don't know who else to call. I can't call Brad. He would blab to the world about my mistake, but even if he didn't, he knew nothing about vehicles.

"Hello, Tony and Son, how can I help you?" Jasper nearly yells into the phone.

I laugh. "You almost sound professional."

"Well, I kind of have to. If not, I wouldn't get any business to pay for any of my father's debt."

"Ouch."

I can hear his lips form into a grin. "I didn't think I was ever going to hear back from you."

"Oh, you know, I'm just trying to be the one that got away."

"Double ouch."

My forehead falls onto the wheel again, and this time I tightly shut my eyes and begin to almost whine. "I know, I suck as a friend. It's been a long week," I say. "And I was supposed to call you. I'm sorry."

"Nah," he says. "Don't be. I know you're busy. Playing pretend and all."

"I'm sure I can tell you all about it soon," I lightly smile.

"How soon?"

"Well." My nose wrinkles up, embarrassed. How shitty am I for only calling him when I need something from him? I'm beginning to sound more and more like my father. "Can you help me out?"

His tone suddenly changes. Pure curiosity runs through him. "Are you okay?"

"No, no. I'm fine. I just broke down on the side of the road and didn't know who else to call. No one is as smart as you when it comes to vehicles."

"Now you are just trying to butter me up, darlin'."

"No, I swear. Everyone is too high on their horses to give two shits about learning how to do anything simple in life. They just throw their money at someone and tell them to do it. Otherwise, it's a waste of time."

"Hm. I'll call my best tower to come to get you, but you better watch it. He's a real flirt."

"You sound almost worried, Mr. Smith."

He chuckles. "Nah, Connor would never hurt a fly. He's a good guy. Tell me where you are so I can send him your way."

Now

Connor

It's been two hours since I left Lillian's side, and I regret every minute. I shouldn't have let my feelings toward her father push me away from her. She needs me, now more than ever.

If Jasper was awake, he would laugh at me and say, "Come on, kid. Get your shit together."

I wish he was awake. I wish he was in my position and I was in his. He doesn't deserve to be lying in the bed while his soon-to-be wife is awake without the knowledge of his existence. It should be him telling the story of their love, not me. He knows certain details I don't because it was none of my business to know them.

But I'm trying my best.

I sit on the bathroom counter, swinging my legs as I stare down at the freshly mopped tile. I don't know what to do. It's still storming outside, and I don't want to leave the building.

She is leaving in a few days. I have until then to convince her of a different life. Even if she doesn't believe me, just keeping her company is enough. She doesn't seem to mind it. At least, I don't think so. She's always been blunt about things. If she had a problem with me, she would have said something by now.

I lift my arm and check my calculator watch. I wonder if they are still there after an hour. Even if they are, I might just have to put up with their presence until they leave.

I jump off the counter and exit the bathroom, heading for the elevator. A smile forms on my lips as I watch her father exit the elevator. Thankfully, he doesn't see me but continues looking down at his phone and goes about his business as he leaves the hospital.

He's leaving alone, I realize. *But where's Brad?*

Without hesitation, I continue on my journey up to their floor and to her room. While passing the nurse's station, I notice a familiar face leaning over the counter. The nurses giggle at his words. He's probably saying something like, "You know, I used to be a football player? Yeah, I could have gone pro, but my heart just couldn't leave my pretend girlfriend behind." Or some shit like that. Despite their gaze, he doesn't look up, and I creep past, squeezing myself into the door crack and closing it behind me.

"There you are!" Her voice flutters in my stomach. "Where did you go?"

"I had to take a breather." I snatch the book from my chair and sit down, taking a deep breath before looking her in the eyes. Her cheeks are flushed, and her eyes are red from crying. "What's wrong?"

She groans and throws her head back against her pillows. "Everything is so overwhelming."

I nod. "I can imagine."

"Brad is talking about our future, and my father… apparently has big plans." After a moment of silence, she turns her head toward me. "I want to meet Jasper."

That flutter returns. "Really? You really want to?"

She nods with a grin. "I have to meet him. It'll put a face to the story. Maybe even remember. Don't you think so?"

"I think we can make that happen. I don't see why not?"

I don't see a problem with her seeing him. The biggest issue is her father. I'm not sure if he gave them specific instructions on her care and his wishes, but I'm determined to ruin them. Especially for Jasper.

"Give me a second. I need to find your doctor first."

"He's not going to let me go," she pouts. "Why can't we just sneak off?"

I grab her hand and lightly squeeze it. "You know why, Lil. Right now, we have to play by your father's rules. Otherwise, I have no chance of trying to save your memory from being completely erased."

She nods and relaxes.

She trusts me. She trusts my judgement. Even if I'm not in the right state of mind to make those types of judgements.

I brush her hair back from her forehead and kiss her head. "It'll be okay."

I love this girl. I do admit I have an infatuation with her, but that's all it ever was and will always be. An infatuation. She will never be mine, and I'm okay with that. She's Jasper's old lady.

Slipping from her grip and out into the hallway, I notice the nurse's station is quiet. Brad finally left.

After a few seconds of stalking the hallway, I find her doctor. It takes a minute to convince him to let her see Jasper, but he consents to it finally. "We are supposed to respect the rules her father gave us. Especially the one where he specifically told my staff not to let her see Jasper, but I don't see the harm in it. I don't know the type of person Jasper is, but I know the type of person Mr. Abernathy portrays... Please let a nurse help you get her down the hallway," he says. "Connor?"

"Hm?"

"This could be good for both of them. But God only knows."

God only knows.

It was hard to put my faith in God right now. It seems like He already has so much on His plate. I mean, everyone in this damn hospital is probably trying to ask Him for a miracle. It would be selfish of me to ask for one, too. Especially when the world is already going to shit. He has better things to do.

❊ ❊ ❊

A nurse helps Lillian out of the bed and into a wheelchair, pushing her down the hall and into Jasper's room. The nurse pushes her close to Jasper's side and then leaves the room.

Lillian sits quietly in her chair. Her eyes steadily watch in almost amazement, a bit curiously. She lets out a small gasp, finding herself short of breath.

"He is nothing like I pictured him to be," she says silently.

I circle the bed opposite of her. I lean my back against the window. "How did you picture him, then?"

"Ugly," she banters. "I don't know. Not this. Not handsome. He is well put together. He's something out of a magazine, Connor."

Laughter pours out of my mouth. "I'm sorry to disappoint you. I don't know how to describe a 'handsome' man. To me, he's just a goofball with plain features."

"He is not plain."

I take a deep breath and watch as she stands from her chair, sitting next to him in bed. She's hesitant but begins to run her fingers over his knuckles, then leans forward and brushes his hair away from his forehead. Her hand hovers over his cuts and bruises as if she wants to touch them.

She gulps quietly. "How did it happen? The car accident."

"I can't tell you yet."

"Why not?"

"Your story isn't finished. I can't spoil the end."

She huffs. "Well, obviously it's not a very good ending if we end up in a car accident and I lose my memory."

"Who said your story stops there?" a familiar voice interrupts.

I suck on my bottom lip as I watch Lillian's face turn toward the door. Jasper's mother enters, pulling a sweater over her shoulders and crossing her arms over her chest. Her teeth chatter from the cold air.

"Hi, Lillian. How are you, sweetie?" she asks. "I didn't mean to interrupt your time with him."

"It's okay," she drawls. Her voice shakes with nerves. "You look just like him."

She nods and leans against the doorframe. She plays with a necklace that is tightly wrapped around her neck. "I get that a lot, but honestly, he has his father's face. It's sometimes hard to look at him."

Lillian turns her head toward Jasper again. "Can you read to me here, Connor?" she asks. "I want to be with him."

The stress that I had from earlier melts away as her words echo inside my brain. Even if she doesn't remember him, she wants to be near him. Maybe she finds comfort in him through her story. Maybe I'm wrong about Brad.

Like everything else, she plays pretend when it comes to her father.

Then

Lillian

I push myself off the side of my car as the tow truck comes into view. The large vehicle pulls off to the side of the road after passing me. He backs the tail end of his vehicle to the front of mine and then cuts the engine.

A foot pushes the door open with a swift kick, and a skinny man jumps out the door. His jeans are rolled up around his ankles, his once-white Converse are now covered in mud and dirt. His feet samba to a beat as he comes closer.

He pulls his headphones out of his ears, then uncovers his eyes and pushes his black sunglasses onto the top of his head, brushing his dirty blond hair back. "Lillian, right?"

"Yup. That's me."

His blue eyes scan my car for a second before asking, "What's her name?"

"What?"

"What's your car's name? Everyone names their car."

"What?" I laugh. "I don't know. I haven't thought about it before."

"Women," he says, as he shakes his head. He breaks into a smile and then motions me to follow him. "Climb into my truck. I'll give you a lift to the shop. Jasper is expecting you."

After a few moments of watching Connor hook the back of the truck up to the front of my car, he lifts the vehicle onto the back of his. He climbs into the cab, slams the door, and puts the truck in drive.

He pats the steering wheel. "Forgive me, but the radio doesn't work."

"That's alright."

My hair whips around from the wind, and the windows are down. Some strands stick to my lips, my tongue tangling in some. I pick the strands away from my face, and my finger searches the door for the window button.

"That doesn't work, either… nor the heat or air conditioning." The crack in his voice showed that I embarrassed him for driving a piece of junk.

I smiled lightly. "I think it would be simpler to tell me what works."

"Yeah, well, my father tries his best. He enjoys the job, though. So do I, most of the time. You won't believe some of the crazy shit I see."

I don't reply.

"I'm Connor, but I guess you already know that."

"Lillian Abernathy."

After a moment of silence and a few road detours, he blurts out, "You're the Lillian!"

"The Lillian? There are other Lillians in this town?"

"Well… My grandmother's name was Lillian."

"What? Really?"

"No, but you never know. Right?"

This kid is weird. "How old are you? Like, are you old enough to be driving this thing around?"

He laughs. "The same age as you, I think. Eighteen. Jasper told me that you were a spicy one."

"Oh, did he?"

"He might have warned me about your sharp tongue." His smile fades. "Don't take it to heart. Please? He likes you, and it would kill me if I ruined anything between you."

My heart flutters. He must have talked a great deal about me to his friend. "Connor," I interrupt his rambling. "You didn't say anything wrong. My gosh, boy, you need some self-confidence."

"I have some." His brow lowers.

"No, no, you don't. You sound like a girl that apologizes for everything."

"I have confidence." He slams on the brakes at a stop sign and rubs the leather steering wheel. "Just not around beautiful women."

I cross my arms and get comfortable in the cut-up leather seats. "Gosh, are you always such a suck-up?" I mutter.

He laughs. "Are you always such a bitch?"

"Always."

Maybe he wasn't so weird after all.

❀ ❀ ❀

The shop is busy, but that doesn't surprise me. Jasper is the type of person that I would trust to work on my vehicle. He gives fair prices and doesn't fuck you over, trying to sell something to you that you don't need.

Connor pulls down the drive and off to the side, into the grass. He doesn't want to block anyone in when the parking lot is not very big. "Well, Lillian, this has been so much fun. We should do it more often," he says.

"Smart ass."

"Hey! You can say a lot about my ass, but at least I don't have a stick-up mine. I don't know how Jasper can put up with you," he fires back. "You are ridiculous."

"I don't know, either. Honestly."

I don't take his comment personally. I know I have a way of getting underneath people's skin. Half of the time, I deserve the reaction.

Before I can reach for the door handle, Jasper beats me to it. Wearing a big grin and a dirty white shirt, he says, "Hello, darlin'. Did Connor play nice?"

"Did I?" I hear him whisper.

"He was a doll," I say, as I slip out of the truck. "He's really sweet."

"Who's the kiss ass now?" he whispers again, snickering.

"Hopefully not too sweet... Thank you, Connor!" He shuts the door behind me and walks beside me to his shop. "Park her wherever you see the room, we are slammed today."

"Is it usually like this?"

"Sometimes. It's nice, though."

"But you work alone…"

He doesn't continue the conversation. Instead, he changes the subject. "You didn't call me as you promised."

"When did I promise you that?"

We stop at the bay doors. "The night you got very drunk."

I shrug, slightly laughing. "I have no idea what you are talking about," I smirk, acting coy. "Darlin'."

The man's rough and greasy face lights up. "You rascal. You do remember."

"Maybe."

"How about tonight? A motorcycle ride and a nice plate of dinner? What do you say?" His country accent grows thick. He's excited. "I believe you owe me a story."

The thought of the football game and dinner with Brad's family comes to mind. Disappointment hits me, and the light inside slowly fades away.

"I can't."

"Why not?"

"I have to have dinner with Brad's parents later."

The smile on his dimpled face fades. "Why? Why on earth would you want to do that?"

"I don't. You know that, but I have to."

"Then, don't go. You don't have to do anything with those crazy people."

"You don't know the consequences if I don't."

"And if you do? You're just supposed to sell your life away to people who don't give a shit about you? To people who only look at you as a prize or a heifer that's only good for breeding?"

If this was anyone else, I would take offense to his words, but deep down, I know he means well and is only making a point. He cares.

My lips form a grin, a light laugh pouring out. "Did you just compare me to a cow?"

His face relaxes, and his shoulders drop. "I-I didn't mean to. You know I didn't."

"If I'm a cow, you're a jackass."

"Hey!"

A squeal escapes my lips as he wraps his arms around my torso and picks me up. My legs thrash, but my heart wants this badly. To play. To escape.

He's different. I've never known love or kindness. Brad never shows me this and neither does my father. We don't joke. We don't play. We don't laugh. Happy is out of the question.

In the meantime, Connor unhooks my Beetle from his truck and leaves it in a line of cars. He parks his truck elsewhere and comes to join. "Here are her keys, Jasper. I put it with the others that you have lined up for the day."

Jasper licks his lips as he looks up at me. My head falls toward him, and our foreheads graze. He slowly lowers me and sighs, "Thank you, Connor." He takes the keys from him and rubs the back of his neck with his hand. "Are you still coming over for dinner tonight?"

"Wait, what?" My mouth slightly falls open. "I thought you were just begging me to go out with you?"

He snaps his head back to me, "I am, I mean, I'm still hoping you will change your mind, but I know you probably won't. I know you can't change those types of plans, and I have to feed Connor somehow."

"Anna makes the best chicken and dumplings," Connor chimes in. "Just saying."

"Connor's father is usually busy all day, so he comes over for dinner a lot of the time."

Connor shrugs. "My mother works nights stocking at the local grocery store, so she usually sleeps during the day. Usually, Mrs. Smith sends me home a plate for her so she can eat before she goes to work."

"That's sweet of Jasper's mother."

"She's an angel. She's like a second mother, honestly."

Besides the attraction between Jasper and me, it's nice to be around someone normal and wholesome. Even Connor. People with compassion and empathy. Not toxic and distasteful. I envy people like them.

What's it like to wake up without being on edge? Is your jaw relaxed? I bet it doesn't ache from being clenched all the time. What's it like to have family gatherings? I honestly forget what it's like. To be able to look at someone without thinking the worst of them?

Just normal people.

I crave it.

"Oh, I would hate to interrupt. It sounds lovely."

Jasper's face falls, and he inches toward me. "No, no. If you change your mind, I can always change plans," he assures me. "Connor won't mind going home alone. Hell, some nights he has to because I sometimes work late."

I look at Connor. His lips are slightly parted as he stands in disbelief. You could tell he was looking forward to tonight.

"Right?" Jasper looks back at him.

"Right."

I clench my teeth and rock on the heels of my feet. "Okay. I'll go call Brad then."

Jasper's face lights up. "What are you going to tell him?" "Brad?" Connor's face twists into confusion. "Brad, who?"

I ignore Connor. Jasper can fill him in on the unusual situation that is called my life. I'm a bit surprised that Jasper left that detail out, but continued to still speak highly of me. I wonder what he said to Connor.

"I don't know. That I got hit by a bus?" I laugh. "I honestly don't know. Something. So, you better think of somewhere good to eat."

"Yes, ma'am!"

"Who's Brad?" Connor continues. Hatred filled in his voice. Obviously annoyed because he is getting ignored by both of us now.

I step aside for a moment, walking back to my car. I scroll through the many text messages that Brad has left me and decide to call him. Knowing he is probably in class or the gym, I quickly grow embarrassed. I didn't want to get him in trouble.

It rings for the fifth time. Then, he answers.

"Hello? Lil?" his voice is almost in a whisper. "Where the hell are you?"

"My car broke down."

He groans. "I told you to get rid of that piece of shit months ago."

"I'm not calling to fight with you," I remind him. "I'm calling you to let you know that I won't be able to make it to dinner tonight."

"You're not calling me to fight with me, but you want to start a fight by telling me you aren't coming to my parents' dinner? Make that make sense, Lillian."

"I could have just not called, but I thought that since I have more respect for you that I would act like an adult and call you to let you know."

I slam my back against the car, the anger inside swirling. My guard was up, and I waited patiently for an answer.

"What excuse are you using this time?"

"Well, my car—"

"I can come to pick you up."

"I just got my period."

"I have ibuprofen at home."

"One of my father's rat dogs died."

"Oh, did it? I'm so sorry," he exaggerates. "You hate those dogs, and you hate your father, so I doubt you will be grieving."

"Alright, well, something came up. I'm not coming. End of discussion."

"Fine, Lillian. This is going to look bad and suspicious—"

I hang up before I have to hear any more of his rant.

Then

Jasper

Is she honestly the type of girl you want to take home to your mother? She is nothing like Skylar. She's a terrible human being," Connor complains. He narrows his bright eyes at me, his eyelashes a tint of red. His freckled cheeks are flushed and sweaty from the late summer heat. "Your mother is going to hate her."

"That is what I like about her. She's nothing like Skylar. I don't need another Skylar because, frankly, there will never be someone like her. There will ever only be one Skylar in this universe, and I had the pleasure of calling her mine. But she's gone now."

"I know, but you know what I meant."

"I know what you meant. You don't know that girl like I do."

"You don't know that girl at all, Jasper. You only met her about a week ago! Sure, you knew her back in high school, but that was ages ago, and she didn't give a rat's ass about you then. She was too high on her horse to get to know you."

"Connor, I have a good feeling about her. Just let me see this one through. Please?"

"And who the hell is Brad? She's not talking about Brad Taylor, is she?"

"Yes, she is. And it's complicated."

"Complicated? Do you know how dangerous the Taylor and Abernathy families are? They run this whole fucking town, Jasper. That means she's dangerous. She's off-limits. Don't fuck with her."

"Are you done?"

"No, and another thing. What about your son?"

"Connor."

"What is he going to think?"

"Okay, I get it. You want to protect me and my family, but seriously… It's fine. No one is replacing Skylar. No one will ever replace her. She is the mother of my child, and I will always love her. And I don't plan on having Lillian meet Greyson just yet. Lillian and I are just having fun at the moment, and if it turns into something serious, then yes, but eventually, I do want to get married again," I sigh. After a long minute of silence and Connor's puppy dog face, I can't handle it anymore. "Dammit, Connor. I loved her. I wanted more than ever to keep her. I can't control what happens. And every day I think of what I could have done differently, but the fact is that I couldn't have changed a thing. I have Greyson. That is the best gift that Skylar could have given me."

"I loved her too, you know?" he mumbles. "She was my sister."

My heart sinks, and for a split second, I think he's going to cry. I grab his arm and pull him into my chest, wrapping my arms around his fragile body. It's been hard on his family, and I've tried my best to support them all, but the truth is that they are all equally falling apart in their own ways.

"It's just hard to imagine you with someone else," he continues.

"Don't you think she would want me to be happy? To find someone who will make our son just as happy? To find him a female influence?"

"I know," he muffles into my shoulder. "I know... It's just new."

I pull away. "It's all new. Believe me. I'm scared as hell, too. But I have to put myself out there, or I'll never do it. It's been three years, Connor."

By this time, I hear Lillian's feet shuffle across the gravel as she walks toward us. She had loosened the tie around her neck. "Am I interrupting something?"

"No," I say, as I drop my arms to my side. "Uh, how did it go?"

She scoffs. "The usual. He's a dick."

I can feel Connor's judgement radiating off him. He doesn't understand, and neither do I, but it's obvious that the girl doesn't want to be a part of whatever her daddy is planning for her. She deserves better. She deserves to be free.

I grab a dirty rag from my back pocket and wipe my sweaty brow off. "Alright, give me an hour or two to get some of these customers on their way. I'll close shop for the day, and we will go for a ride into town."

I begin to turn on the heel of my boot to walk into the barn when I hear her voice. "A ride? Like on your motorcycle?"

"I promised you, didn't I?"

She's bashful and silent, then gives a small smile before pushing some strands of her auburn hair behind her ear. Where did the blunt and sassy girl go? She usually would have something smart to say.

"What will you tell your mother?"

"The truth. That she might have to watch Greyson for a little while longer."

"She won't be upset?"

"I don't think so. If anything, probably happy that for once I'm not coming home to mope around in my own misery."

Connor rolls his eyes and steps away, walking back to his truck.

"Is he okay?" She throws her thumb over her shoulder. "He doesn't seem to like me very much."

"He's fine," I chuckle. "That's Skylar's brother. It's just hard for him to see me with someone other than his sister."

"I understand. It was hard to see my father bring home women after my mother died."

"When did she die?"

"It will be three years in December."

I quickly realized what she meant the day we met. People change. She changed herself. She didn't let others change her.

"People change," I nod.

A small smile spreads across her face. "People change."

"I'm so sorry. I didn't realize—"

She shifts her posture. "Jasper, I don't know if you have realized, but I'm not the most pleasant person to be around. I hate the world. I hate the world for taking my mother. I hate the world for leaving me alone. And I simply hate living in a world where she doesn't exist."

A customer comes walking out of the barn. "Jasper, how much longer, son? I have a wedding to get to!"

I turn to look at the elderly man. "Sorry, Mr. Turner. I'm coming."

I spin back to look at Lillian. Her blue eyes are glassy as she reminisces about her mother. I want this conversation to go further, but I can't neglect my customers.

I kick the rocks with my boot. "Please don't disappear on me, darlin'. It might be a bit boring for a little while, but I promise you my full attention later."

I dig into my pockets for change and hand it to her. "Here. Grab yourself a coke while you wait. I promise I won't be long."

The few coins drop into the palm of her hand. She looks down at the change and then back up at me. "Okay."

❀ ❀ ❀

I disappear for a few hours. I change the oil on a few vehicles and knock them out of line, getting them out of the shop. I look at a few vehicles and determine their verdict, reporting back to their owners. But my mind still remains the same—Lillian.

"I'm sorry, Ms. Banks... No, I know... I just have others in line ahead of you." I turn to look at the doorway of my office. Lillian quietly brings in a cup of coffee from the diner across the street and then disappears. "The earliest is Tuesday."

Some days are harder than others. I run the shop as a one-man show, so when we become super busy, it's hard to get everything done in one day. My customers are usually understanding, but many aren't. They like to argue and try to fight me over the price because of the delays. I've thought about hiring help, but I wouldn't have it any other way. It's hard to trust someone. I'd rather do it alone.

By five o'clock, I'm ready to head home. I haven't had anything to eat all day, and my body is starting to ache. I need something in my system other than coffee.

The shop is finally quiet. No one waited around for me to finish, and most of the cars are gone from the gravel parking lot. The ones that are parked are the ones that need more work.

I turn the lights off and lock up the building, finding Lillian sitting in the passenger seat of her beetle. She rummaged through the front trunk of her car and pulled a few shopping bags out.

She had emptied the bags in the driver's seat, the tissue paper balled up. A cigarette is lit in between her fingers, her hand trembling as she stares out into the field. Her pink lips part slightly and a puff of smoke escaped.

"I didn't know you smoked," I say, as I bend down, crossing my arms and setting them onto the window side.

She jumps slightly. Her brain slowly comes back to reality and out of her deep thoughts and emotions. She gulps. "I usually don't." Wiping a tear from her eye with her thumb, she gradually looks at me. "Are you mad?" she asks, almost too quietly.

"No, darlin'. Why would I be? Because I found you smoking?"

She nods. "I don't want you to think I'm something I'm not. I don't drink, and I don't smoke. Unless there's something heavy on my mind. And I know that usually there are things on my mind, like my father and Brad, but those aren't heavy. Not anymore anyway. I've learned to deal with those emotions. But my mother, that's something else. That's something fresh. It's bottled. No one talks about it, and no one talks about her."

"That's the one thing I think I praise my mama for. When my father died, she didn't act like he was never alive. She talks about him daily like she just saw him yesterday. She keeps his memory alive."

She sticks her arm out the window and taps on her cigarette, letting the ash hit the ground, then puts it back to her lips and inhales. "That's how it should be. Any normal family would keep their loved ones alive even after they're gone. Nope, not my father. There's not one single fucking photo up in our house. After her funeral, they disappeared. He wanted her completely gone." She exhales, and the smoke drifts through the air. "And anyone can argue that he's mourning, but no, it's not normal. Not the way my father is going about it."

I shift the conversation, pointing to the empty bags. "Using Daddy's money, huh?" I mock.

She sniffles and wipes her nose on the back of her hand, smiling. She slightly laughs, "Uh, no. Actually, these were my mother's. She went shopping the day she passed. I never went through her things, but it seemed like the right time. I miss her."

"What did you find?"

She inhales one more time before throwing her cigarette out the window, dropping her legs from the dashboard. She climbs out of the vehicle. "Honestly? New Victoria's Secret underwear and two of the same watches."

"That's... disappointing."

Resting her elbow on the surface of the vehicle, she holds the door open. She throws her head back and laughs. "You're not wrong. I have waited so long to know what was in those bags. I was expecting something meaningful or some souvenir. Not something to remind me that my parents had sex."

I grin. "Are you ready for dinner?"

She slams the door and reaches through the open window to retrieve her purse, throwing the strap onto her shoulder. "I am starving," she moans. "I'm nervous about going into town and someone seeing us, but I'm sure it'll be okay."

"It will be. I assure you."

Then

Lillian

I honestly wish that I wore something other than a schoolgirl outfit, but I didn't see my day going like this. By this time, I would probably walk back to my car after a long afternoon at a football game. I would get in and drive to Brad's house for dinner. I would wear my sweaty cheerleader outfit, hoping that I don't stain Mrs. Taylor's white cushioned chair. I would listen to his family gush over him and how he probably scored a few touchdowns. I would deny dessert and then be awkwardly left with his mother as the men go into his father's study to go over next week's moves. Brad's mother has never liked me. She doesn't like anyone. She won't say two words to me. Instead, she would sip on her wine and stare into a space, hoping and maybe praying that I'd just go away.

She isn't very fond of my father, either. In fact, both of Brad's parents hate him. That's the one thing I never understood. Why surround yourself with toxic people who hate you? I get the keep your enemies closer quote, but it would make my life miserable… In fact, it is, and I'm not even the main character in that scenario.

I often wonder what life would be like if my mother were still alive. Would my father still be mayor? Would I still have to be forced to accompany Brad? I don't think so.

I miss her. Not for the obvious reason of how life would have been, but I miss *her*. I miss our long talks and the way she presented herself. She was so feminine and graceful. What every woman desires to be.

She would have loved Jasper. And maybe even Connor. She liked the down-to-earth types. The die-hard types. She probably would have wanted to meet Jasper before our date and maybe even chat with his mother. I'd argue that it would be inappropriate, being that we are both adults, and she would laugh. She wouldn't care. Embarrassing her child was what she lived for.

It often made me curious about how my parents found each other. At one point, my father was happy with life. He had everything he wanted and needed. So, the question still lingers. What happened to make him money hungry?

My mother often hinted at their famous love story. She caught my father's eye one morning when she was running the cash register at a florist shop. His father had died, and his mother sent him to pick up the floral arrangements. "Your father must have ordered flowers from the store every week. He needed an excuse to see me, but I just thought he had a very lucky girlfriend. So, I never connected the dots until he asked me out on a date," she had said one time.

When my mother died, a piece of him died with her.

"Lil? Are you okay?"

Jasper's voice echoes inside my mind, and my eyes blink as I snap out of the endless void. My vision adjusts, and I am standing staring at the cemetery across the street.

She's buried there.

"Yeah, sorry. They buried my mother there. I drive past it almost every day on my way to school, but I haven't visited her since her funeral. You'd think with all the feelings I have toward my father that I would have a tent pitched up by her headstone, but I just can't bring myself to visit her. And I don't know why."

We have just arrived at the restaurant. The motorcycle ride was beautiful, but the cool air nips at my skin. The sun is setting now, and the stars peek through the red and orange atmosphere.

Jasper taught me safety before climbing on and driving off, worried about my well-being. He slightly regretted taking me for a ride dressed the way that I am, but he didn't want to disappoint. And he didn't.

When we arrive, he offers me his jacket a few times, but I honestly don't need it. Even if my lips do quiver when

I speak. My body is shivering, but we're about to go inside. I'll thaw out then.

"Would you like to go see her?"

No.

I watch as he sets his helmet on the leather seat of his motorcycle, his fingertips grazing the surface.

"Right now?"

He shrugs. "Why not?"

Absolutely not.

"Not right now. I wouldn't even know what to say to her. I'm not the same person that I was two years ago. She wouldn't recognize me," I sigh. My view rakes the empty graveyard and the black metal fence that surrounds it. "One day. Just not today… Besides, you don't want to see me ugly cry."

"My daddy is buried there too, so I understand." His head cocks to the side as he points. "He's in the third row to the right. He's the seventh headstone in line. I go there and 'ugly cry,' too. I visit him at least twice a week."

"Twice a week?" I'm baffled. "Well, aren't you a good boy?"

His country accent thickens. "I try to be."

❀ ❀ ❀

We are seated in the center of the restaurant at a small circular table. White cloths cover the surfaces of all the tables, a single candle in the center. White string lights line the dark wooden ceiling, creating almost a starry effect in the darkroom.

A waiter quickly takes our drink order and drops our menus down in front of us, disappearing into the back. It doesn't take me long to search through the menu to realize the type of place this is. A very over-the-top, overpriced restaurant. The type of restaurant my father wouldn't hesitate to go to, and I am pretty sure he has.

I gulp, looking at the prices. Twenty dollars for a steak and one side, thirty for lobster and one side, and fifty for both. It makes me question Jasper's wealth and his intentions.

"Jasper," I nearly whisper. Even though the room isn't busy, I don't want to be rude and draw attention to ourselves.

"Hm?" He doesn't look up from his menu.

"We can't eat here."

His long eyelashes bat themselves at the menu as a wave of confusion hits him and then he looks up at me. "What? Why?"

My menu falls from my hands. "This place is too expensive. I can't let you buy me dinner. This is insane."

He simply stares. "They have the best steak in town here."

"And look at us. I look like something you ordered off of a naughty school girl porn website and you... you..." I slouch down in my chair. I realize that I'm being over dramatic and that I shouldn't be overreacting. By now, I should know that Jasper is not Brad. He doesn't care about the way he looks.

His eyebrow arches. "What's wrong with the way I'm dressed?" He's pulling at his shirt now.

"You're filthy," I lean forward.

"I know I probably should have cleaned up, but... is it an issue?"

"No?"

He grins. "No?"

"No. I, um..."

He rolls his eyes. "Christ, Lillian, spit it out. You're not going to hurt my feelings. I know how high maintenance you are."

Why is it so hard to tell him the truth? It's just simple flirting. How bad can it be? "I like you dirty," I blurt. My cheeks burn, turning a shade of red. Did I just say that?

"Oh yeah?" He winks at me, chuckling slightly.

I rake my fingernails against my scalp, pulling through my strands of hair. "That is not what I meant," I nervously laughed. "I just meant I don't think I could see you in any other attire. All I have seen you in is dirty clothes and boots. Dirty looks good on you, no doubt, but this restaurant just looks like the type to kick you out for not being high class."

"If they had a dress code, they wouldn't have seated us," he gently says, as he stretches an arm out across the table. He turns over his hand, revealing the callouses on his rough hands. "You worry too much. Don't worry about what others think."

I take his hand.

"Please let me just spoil you, darlin'." He begins to look back down at the menu.

I take a deep breath. I should have known better than to open my mouth. When am I going to realize that he isn't like any man that I have ever met? He isn't self-centered or vain. I'm afraid that if I kept comparing him to Brad, the Taylors, the people at school, or my father, I'll lose him.

I pick my menu back up and decide on a chicken Caesar salad. It is still pricey, but just a little less expensive.

"Naughty school girl porn, huh? Can you recommend a good website or…" Without hesitation, I kick his ankle underneath the table. His face wrinkles, and he laughs. "I deserve that."

"Yeah," I snort, laughing.

"So, about that story."

I lift an eyebrow, appearing over the top of the menu. "What story?"

He rolls his eyes and sets his menu down. "You know what story. Don't play mysterious, darlin'. Believe me, you already keep my attention."

I nearly choke as the words leave his mouth. He often makes me feel like my everyday nightmare is dissolving into a dream. He just makes living life fun.

I shut the menu, laying it on the table. I lean to the side and cross my legs, grinning like an idiot. I lick my lips and shake my head. "Why do you want to hear the story so damn bad? It's not even that good."

He scoots his chair closer to the table and leans forward. "Lillian Abernathy being bad? That has to be a juicy story."

I shake my head in disbelief. The story slightly embarrasses me, and I try my best to ignore it. "Brad and I always have had our differences, but every once in a while, we actually get along. A group of our friends got together and just decided to go skinny dipping after long hours at some party. My father and, I would imagine, the Taylors called the cops to come looking for us. That's about it."

"That's it?"

"I told you, it's not a very good story. We were just out really late."

He grins, showing some teeth. He runs a hand through his thick black hair. "A little rebel you are. I didn't think you did things like that."

"I usually don't, but I'd do anything to piss off my father."

❉ ❉ ❉

We were both happy and full. We had too much to eat, our plates being larger than our stomachs. Then, we ended up sharing a slice of apple pie for dessert. Probably not the greatest idea, but it was worth every bite.

With my arm wrapped around his back and his arm draped over my shoulders, we walk together out of the restaurant. My head lays against his shoulder.

I like this feeling—the feeling of this almost being my safety net. I know I shouldn't be diving head-first into whatever this is, but this is becoming almost natural. The more time we spend together, the more I want to be in his presence and near his touch. To hear his voice and smell his cologne.

"What does your son think you're doing right now?" I ask, watching as our feet step at the same pace.

"He thinks I'm out with a friend. We had this discussion the other night. I like to be honest with him and not surprise him with new information."

"How does he feel about it?" All this time together, he doesn't go one second without speaking about his son. I let him tell me things about him, but I don't dare cross any lines. This is the first time I test the waters, seeing where I stand.

"He's okay with it. I think not knowing his mother, he doesn't know really what to think of a female presence. He's around my mama and Connor's mama a lot, but he knows I don't have female friends."

"You don't?"

"No," he shrugs. "Not really. At least not ones I would give my time and attention to."

The sun barely peeks over the horizon, and night has taken its place. The air seems cooler than before, but it's fresh and almost calm. Light posts shine along the empty streets, everyone in the safety of their warm, cozy homes.

Our feet reach the edge of the sidewalk. We've walked the strip and are only feet away from the cemetery now, it lingers on the other side of the street. It's dark and almost scary, the silence eerie.

"I want you to meet my daddy."

I raise my eyes to him. Even with a light post, I can only see parts of his face. Shadows erase the expression from his features, but I can tell by the stern tone in his voice that he's serious. "You do?"

He shifts uncomfortably. "I... yeah. I do. He would have enjoyed your company. I tend to think there are similarities between the two of you."

I grin. "How so?"

"He just loved life. He was stubborn and hardheaded—"

I nudge him with my elbow. "Oh, wow. Thanks."

He chuckles. "Not just that, but he was incredibly smart and witty. He was determined to prove to himself that he could do anything that he set his mind to. He was a dreamer, and he loved with all of his heart."

I smile warmly. "You described my mother."

He looks down at me.

"She was the same way. She was sweet and such an old soul. Loved old movies, music, and cars. She loved to shop at thrift stores and would drag me to garage sales. We would come home with so much crap," I laugh, as the memories appear right in front of me. "My father used to tell her to quit bringing home useless junk, but she always found a place for it. Eventually, our house looked like a museum. My father would remove things slowly over time, but I don't think she ever caught on. Eventually, after she died, he got rid of it all. He hired some private designer and made the house some modern, chic-looking monstrosity," I say. "Everything was spotless and organized. Every picture of my mother was taken down and replaced by professional photographs of random places. Places he never plans to visit. I don't like it. It's annoying and weird."

"He erased her that quickly?"

I nod. "That quickly. All of her art and all her creative junk were gone by the time I came home from school. I had no say in any of it."

He sighs. "I'm sorry."

I pull him closer to me, tightening my grip around him as I attempt to not cry. "It's okay," I choke. "Maybe I do need to see her. Just once."

"We don't have to."

"It's okay. I want to. I miss her."

Then

Lillian

He doesn't rush me. Instead, he waits silently for me to make the first step off the sidewalk. I think deep down he knows that this is a big moment for me and respectfully gives me time to make the first move.

As I step down off the sidewalk, I can't help but second guess myself. This is long overdue, but I can't decide whether or not I'm ready for this. I bite my bottom lip and look toward the starry sky, praying and hoping that I can find the strength to do this.

I step back onto the sidewalk, tears streaming down my face. "Why is visiting my mother so difficult? You would think that I would see her every day because of all the love that I carry for her; but I don't. I pretend like it never happened and talk about her like she is just out on a distant trip. Like she is coming home anytime now," I sob. "Why does He take only the good?"

"I ask myself that almost every day, darlin'."

I'm not sure if I am religious or not. I grew up in a household that was, and I tried my best to understand how to love Him, but ever since my mother's passing, it has been hard. Questioning His sanity isn't necessarily a sin, but it feels like it sometimes. Maybe God and I just don't see eye to eye on things, especially when it comes to planning out my life.

I lick my lips and shiver, a cold chill climbing up through my spine. I rub my hands over my bare arms, attempting to warm up. It doesn't help that I'm walking around in a skimpy skirt, either. I sniffle, my eyes drying.

Jasper notices and snakes his arms out of his gray sweater. "Here," he offers.

My eyes are immediately drawn to his biceps, and I can't help but stare. My cheeks are heating and thawing out quickly. "Oh! Uh, t-thank you," I stutter. I wipe the tears from my cheeks and lightly smile. I pull my purse strap from my shoulder. "What about you?"

"I don't need it," he reassures me, as he helps me into the large sweater and it nearly eats me whole. He readjusts my purse strap back onto my shoulder. "There."

I didn't realize we had that much of a size difference. I knew that he was a bit taller, but this? I find it amusing.

The material is soft and still holds the warmth from his body. On the inside, I'm screaming, enjoying every moment of this, even if I'm about to face one of the biggest challenges of my life.

I have him. That's all that matters, I tell myself.

His cheeks wrinkle as he smiles widely, dimples poking out slightly. I watch as he takes a step back to investigate my new wardrobe.

"What?" I ask.

"Nothing." Jasper shakes his head. "I just think you are beautiful."

My eyes shift toward the ground. I can't look at him. Between my ridiculous smile and the thousands of butterflies that have been unleashed inside of me, I want to burst.

I can't admit to him that he just makes me a better person. That I want to be a better person for him. That somehow this oversized gray sweater makes me feel like a superhero and it acts as my cape. It acts as a shield and protects me from all the worries of the world. Simply, it makes me feel special.

After, silence fills the air between us, then I step off of the sidewalk again. "I think I'm ready." He intertwines our fingers and allows me to lead him across the street to the cemetery. My stomach turns as we enter through the black gates. "Can we visit your father first?"

"Sure, it's just over here."

A sidewalk is paved, creating a winding path through the fairly large graveyard, with light posts scattered to show the trail. They placed the newer tombstones in the front of the cemetery as the older ones are dilapidating from old age toward the back, lining the forest's edge. A large stone angel sits in the center, surrounded by benches and pretty trees.

The wind howls through the trees, wrestling the leaves. It almost sounds like a lullaby. One that only answers death's call.

"Creepy is just one of the words that I would use to describe this place," I say, as I watch my footing.

"I'll protect you from Casper, the friendly ghost," he half laughs.

"Not funny."

"Oh, don't tell me you believe in ghosts."

"I don't know what to believe, honestly."

Jasper leads me off of the paved trail and into one of the many rows of headstones. The farther we follow the row, the farther we are from the light. Once we get to the seventh headstone, we stop.

Even in complete darkness, I can see the frown that has appeared on his face. "Hey, Pop. How are you?" he says, as he kneels. He puts his hand on the stone and then leans forward to kiss it. "I brought you a visitor."

I press my knees against the freshly cut grass and find myself rubbing my hand down his back. "It's nice to meet you, sir."

Silence.

Something inside of me tells me to stay silent, almost as if he's mentally talking to his father. Things he can't say out loud. I respect that.

Once he's done and the silence has been filled with the sound of crickets, he rises onto his feet and then helps me up. He wipes a few tears away from his eyes.

"Are you okay?" I reach for his hand.

"It's moments like these where I wish he wasn't six feet under the ground."

In a sense, I felt almost awkward. My heart hurt for Jasper, but I couldn't find the words to comfort him. There are no words for comfort in these kinds of situations. I barely can find comfort within myself when it comes to my mother.

He takes a deep breath and then nods toward the cemetery. "Do you remember where she is resting?"

Emotion isn't something that I planned to indulge in today, but it's too late. I already agreed to it.

I blink for a moment and look out beyond the many stones. It breaks my heart that this is all there is to life. That this is what is waiting at the end of our journey. Death and an empty graveyard. "I think so," I nod, as I pull him behind me.

I lead him back to the lit pathway, my palms sweating. My heart pounds against my chest, and I instantly want to throw up.

We pass a few more rows and then I pull him off the path. And once again, we are welcomed by the darkness and pulled away from the light. The darkness consumes us.

Once we are at the correct headstone, I stop and stare down at it. His hand squeezes mine a few times, but he stays silent.

I turn to look at him. "What do I even say to her? What do you usually say to your father?"

"I talk to him as if he's sitting across the table from me. I tell him everything that he has been missing, even if he obviously knows about it already because I'd like to think that they watch everything that we do. It's just comforting to talk to them about anything heavy on your heart."

I consider his words and turn back toward her stone. "Hi, Mama. It's been a minute," I start. I gulp, my eyes beginning to sting as I become flustered with emotion. "I'm sorry I don't visit. It's just too damn hard."

A tear rolls down my cheek, and I glance over at Jasper as he nods in approval.

I clear my throat. "You'd hate the world that we live in today. I'm sure you've noticed all the pain that Father has caused, but in a way, I don't blame him. I know his intentions are supposed to be good, but he's going about it all in the wrong ways. Life was simpler when you were here... I miss you."

I silently wish to see a sign—something that shows me that she's still here, listening to my every word.

Is she evening listening?

I let go of Jasper's hand and wipe away the tears. "They seem to be taking care of her headstone," I say, chewing on my lip as I squat down. My hand grazes the front of it, outlining the chalky engraving of her name.

"Yeah, they take really good care of the cemetery. They always wash off the tombstones and cut the grass every week—"

His words become a distant noise as my eyes fix on a freshly cut bouquet of red roses. It's slightly propped against the bottom of her stone, the petals still soft and bright. My hand reaches down to touch them, but I quickly stop myself. "Who would bring my mother flowers?" I ask myself out loud. "It couldn't possibly be my father, could it?"

"If not him, then maybe a friend?" Jasper chimes in.

"Maybe," I shrug. "I'm glad someone has been visiting her because I've been a selfish daughter."

Just as I'm about to continue, my phone rings. I rise to my feet and dig into my purse, retrieving it.

Devin.

I groan, frustrated already. I don't have to answer the phone to know what he plans to say to me. He doesn't just call me for no reason.

Jasper's eyes search my face. The smile fades from his face. "What's wrong?"

"He manages to always ruin something for me," I murmur. I answer the call and hold the phone up to my ear. "What?"

Devin coughs abruptly into the phone. "He's here again."

I sigh, pinching the bridge of my nose. I shake my head. "For how long this time?"

"Since opening."

Lunchtime.

117

"I'll be there in a second. I'm only a block or two away."

"Thank you, Lillian."

I shove my phone back into my purse and bite my lip, scared to even make eye contact with Jasper. "I'm so sorry," I squeak. "I have to go."

"Is everything okay?" He steps forward and tucks a few strands of hair behind my ear, his fingers combing through my auburn hair. He cups the back of my head. His face is now inches away from mine.

It's usually easy for me to hide my feelings, but I can't hide from him. He reads me like an open book.

I suck on my bottom lip, and all the anger suddenly slips away. "My father goes to the bar down the street from time to time, which is fine, but he tends to overstay his welcome and refuses to go home. It's just not the greatest look for a mayor."

He licks his lips. "It shouldn't have to be your responsibility to clean up his mess."

"I know, but no one else is going to do it. He only starts to drink when he is thinking of my mother… which recently has become more frequent."

I know he doesn't understand. Neither did I half the time, but he's my father. It's an instinct to always help him out of any messy situation.

"Alright, just promise me you will call me as soon as you get home. I need to know that you're safe." His hand cups the back of my head.

"Alright, I will."

I stand on my tippy toes and quickly peck his lips. Once my feet are back flat on the pavement, I realize what I've done. I kissed him. Everything just felt so normal. As if we've been dating for years and I'm only leaving him for a second.

But we aren't. That was our first kiss and our only kiss.

I gasp, covering my mouth with my hand. "I-I am so sorry," I fumble with my words. "I don't know why—"

His blue eyes seem to smile down at me. Even in the dark, the nearby light post glistens in the depth of them. A shimmer of blue and green swirls together, a glint in the center. His hands move to my jaw, and he clutches tight, pulling me back to his lips.

His lips are soft and delicious. His breath is heavy against mine as our lips wrestle against each other. My hands trace the bottom of his shirt as I tug slightly, my eyes tightly closed.

"Oh! Your sweater." I pull away slightly.

He shakes his head. "Keep it. I'll get it from you the next time I see you. Stay warm, and call me when you get home."

Then

Lillian

I'm embarrassed and, frankly, ashamed. There's never a dull moment in my life, and I'm tired of it. If I never find the love of my life or a soulmate in a friendship, I wouldn't mind being completely alone.

I only want to be alone.

It doesn't help that this is becoming a weekly routine. He can't take care of himself anymore. He's tried, but it's obvious that he's failing and falling apart. Guilt eats him from the inside out, and he doesn't bother trying to hide it. And it's ruining his reputation as a mayor. I wish he would admit to himself that he needs help.

My feet stop as I reach The Local Bar. Voices and music slip through the crack at the bottom of the door, and the lights are dimmed. The building is an old red brick building, and it holds no windows, perfect for those who stay until the sun comes up, but bringing instant regret as they flee from the sheltered dark and enter the sunlight.

I pull at the golden knob and enter the crowded room. Laughter pours from the corner with the sound of pool balls colliding. The rainbow jukebox blares a song by Led Zeppelin.

It's hard to see everyone's faces. My father could stand inches away from me, and I wouldn't even notice. The thick fog from everyone smoking cigarettes makes the inside eerie and almost nauseating. I hate these environments. Especially when everyone is intoxicated.

"Hey!" a voice booms. My head whips to the bar. The bartender stands at the end, polishing a glass. Pounds of makeup surround her dark eyes. "You can't be in here. No kids allowed."

She doesn't give me time to answer.

She clicks her tongue against the top of her roof. "What? Are you fucking deaf? Get the fuck out."

"I'm just here to find someone. Then, I'm leaving, I promise!" I scream over the loud music. I move closer to the bar, and the lingering eyes of strange men watch my every move.

"Veronica!" Devin screams. "Shut the fuck up. I called her."

Devin's rounded body appears next to her. He leans over and whispers something in her ear, making her smug face fall. Her eyes dart back at me, then roll to the back of her head in disbelief.

"Sorry," she mouths before walking away.

His hairy arm hits the counter before leaning over and pointing to the back corner. "He's back there," he says. His voice is scratchy and desperately needs to be cleared out. "It is becoming a weekly thing. It's not a good look for our town if he keeps this up. Get him out of here, and get him some help."

My eyes follow his finger. My father sits alone, huddled in a booth in the corner of the room. He stacked empty shot glasses into a pyramid and placed them perfectly in front of him on the table.

"He's not causing any harm, is he?" I snap, without looking at the bar.

It irritates me. This shouldn't have to be my responsibility. He's a grown man. It's his reputation that he's ruining, not mine.

His mouth slightly parts. "No, but he's the mayor. He shouldn't be in here every Friday night. Now, if he wants to drown himself in whiskey at home, that's his business, but it's everyone's business once it's inside my bar. Got it?"

I sigh and pinch the bridge of my nose as I attempt to not cry. I'm tired. Beyond tired.

Legally, I can move out now that I'm eighteen. Hell, in the state of Georgia, I could have moved out at seventeen, but as much as my father forces me to have a life, he doesn't want me to get a job. He wants cheerleading, school, and Brad to be priority. A father expecting a boy to be a priority? Psh.

The smell of cigarettes fills my nose as I push past a group of bikers. A nauseating wave washes over me, the stench too overwhelming. I push closer to my father's corner. His body is still hunched over the table.

I bite my lip, not ready to disturb the beast. I know what is to come.

I tap his shoulder and watch as his face slowly turns to face me, his eyes bloodshot and wide. "What do you want?"

I point over my shoulder. "It's time to go. They are kicking you out… again."

"I just got here!"

The pyramid of shot glasses says otherwise, but I'm not going to argue.

I shrug. "Take it up with the bartender. He is the one that called me to come to get you."

He groans, "I'm not doing anything wrong. I'm simply sitting here and keeping to myself. You're lying. Leave me alone."

"I'm not lying," my voice rises. "Get up. You can't be here. You're the mayor. Remember? You have to look like a family man. Not a depressed asshole drinking his life away." I pull at his elbow, but he doesn't budge. Instead, he grins and begins to laugh at me.

"Get out of my face, Lillian," he warns. "Now."

"No, not until you come home. They don't want you here, James." It feels weird saying my father's name, like a sour candy tickling my tongue.

He laughs and throws his head back as he swallows another shot. "You have no right talking to me that way." He stares at his handmade pyramid, his lips forming a firm line. "You're just skipping school now. Skipping dinner with the Taylors? Why?"

Shit.

"Throwing it all away? All the bullshit I had to go through to make sure your life was picture perfect. Throwing it away, and for what?" His voice grows louder. The music is becoming a distant noise now. "Some trashy kid?"

"Father—"

His hand raises, and he stops me. His green eyes send an icy shiver down my spine. "Oh. You didn't think I would find out? In my fucking town, Lillian."

My heart stops. This is it. I couldn't see Jasper anymore, and he's going to make sure of it.

His hand balls into a fist, and he hits the table, the pyramid falling. The shot glasses hit the table and shatter. I wince at the sound of the glass, but he doesn't budge.

"You are trying to take this away from me. You are trying to ruin this for both of us. Why? I have given you everything your little heart desires. You're whole fucking life. You couldn't follow some simple rules and live life the way I intended it? Why? Why is it so hard?"

A waitress comes to pick up the mess.

"Grab me another few shots," he orders before she leaves. "Thank you."

My jaw is clenched, and the anxiety inside of me is running wild. "I don't know what you are talking about." the words tremble from my lips. *A lie, Lillian? That's the best you can do?*

"Cut the shit. You are not to see that Smith kid. Do you understand? I don't care if you love him or if you are getting some dick from him. Stop whatever it is. Got it? We have an agreement to keep. We owe the Taylors. And I'll be damned if you ruin this for the both of us."

"I didn't agree to anything. You did that."

"Yes, I did. So, stop acting like a slut like your mother and—"

The words twist my insides, and I squeeze my eyes shut, shaking my head. My head cocks to the side, opening my eyes, and I breathe. "Do not say that about her. She was your loving wife and the mother of your child. You were happily married. Why would you say that about her?"

The waitress brings another tray of shots, leaving before he can order any more.

"Nothing. Nothing is just as it seems. Alright, sweetie?" He picks up a shot.

My teeth grind against each other, anger tolling through me. I'm not a kid anymore.

I grab the shot from his hand and throw it at the wall next to his head. He ducks, his eyes wide and his lips parted. "What are you hiding? Why all the secrets? Why all the lies? Tell me!" I nearly scream.

At this point, all eyes are on us now, and the bar is quiet. I can feel the hair on the back of my neck stand from all the attention, but I don't care. I don't care anymore, and I think my father is finally realizing this.

"Enough, sweetie. You're drawing attention to us now. We don't need that."

"I don't give a shit," I spit. I slide into the booth in front of him and grab a few shots. I throw my head back and knock them down, slamming the empty glasses onto the table's surface. "Drink the rest and then you are going to tell me everything you fucking know."

The bitter substance doesn't settle well with my stomach, and I am left with a sour aftertaste. This isn't my first rodeo with whiskey, though. A mixture created for those who wish to erase memories but only create toxic ones.

His tongue glides across the bottom of his lip as he thinks. He thinks about the secrets and the things he wants to say, but he doesn't. Instead, he studies the three remaining glasses in front of him and finishes them.

"Not here," he says before rubbing his legs with the palm of his hands.

"Yes. Here. Now." My pointer finger hits the table repeatedly.

"Not. Here." He slides out of the booth and grabs me by the arm, pulling me up from the leather seat. Without another word, he drags me through the crowded bar and outside into the chilly night.

"Ow!" I yell, as I snatch my arm away. "I'm not a child anymore. I can handle whatever it is you have to say."

He paces in front of me, clearly upset. "You are still a child. Only a child would act like this. Only a child would cheat on their spouse or future partner."

"I didn't cheat."

I didn't. I couldn't have if there was no relationship to begin with. I wanted to try to work things out, but only because I thought I had no other options in the matter. But I can't live under his control anymore.

He stops and steps closer, inches away from my face. "No? When are you going to get it through your thick skull? I have people all around this damn town. They follow you, and they keep their eye on you at all times. I know about your homecoming night. I know about your date earlier today. I know about your car breaking down, and he was the very first person that you fucking called to rescue you," he nearly screams. His breath is heavy and smells of liquor. "So, you tell me the fucking definition of cheating, Lillian. Because while you are fooling around with this boy, Brad is waiting at home for you."

My heart sinks, and my eyes water. The knot in my chest tightens as I struggle to keep my composure. He doesn't scare me, and I know he wouldn't hurt me, but his words cut me like knives that leave me out to die. I bite my lip and struggle to look my father in the eyes. He's angry and hurt. This is personal. Everything he is saying is too personal. "This isn't about me. This is about you, isn't it?"

He sighs and takes a step back, his face falling in disappointment. He rubs the back of his neck. Even in the dark, I can hear him sniffle, the moonlight shining on his eyes as he cries. "Your mother had an affair right before she died. She ruined our family. Not me."

I gasp, and my hands cover my lips. "You're lying."

"Why would I lie to you? Have I ever lied to you before?"

I stay silent.

His large hand reaches out and grabs my jaw, his fingers outlining it. He pulls me to look at him. His tongue licks his teeth. "Look at me when I am talking to you," he growls. "Do I ever fucking lie to you?"

I begin to shake. "No," I huff. My chest is rising and falling quickly.

His eyes drop down to my body. He throws his head back and laughs, his eyes darting back to mine. "Who does that fucking sweater belong to? I've never seen you wear it."

I don't say anything.

He tightens his grip. "It's his, isn't it?"

"Yes," I muffle.

He throws my head back, letting me free. "Throw it away."

I rub the sore spot around my neck. "No."

"No?"

"No. It's just clothing. A piece of fabric."

He steps forward. His forehead wrinkles, and the vein in his neck pops out as he grits his teeth. "It's his piece of fabric, Lillian. How do you think Brad would feel knowing his girlfriend is wearing someone else's clothing?"

I wish I could say that I don't care, but I'm tired of arguing and scared.

"Don't be like your mother, Lillian."

I squeeze my eyes shut and begin to peel the warm sweater away from my bare skin, dropping it to the ground. It hurts me, and, frankly, it feels disrespectful.

"Good. Now, let's go home."

Now

Connor

The days seem to blur together, and the more I read to Lillian, the more I realize that their relationship wasn't so happy in the beginning. It was tough, but they fought hard for one another. I keep praying that one of these days she stops me from reading and tells me the rest of the story herself, but as the days draw on, my faith wanes.

It doesn't help that Brad and her father become regulars. The more they speak to her about the life they wanted her to live, the more she erases the story of Jasper from her mind. She's almost happy to be living her old life, and I'm in disbelief.

I hate it. My breath is useless, and I feel like a waste of space.

Every night, I run home and fill my notebook with memories of the life she lived before us. The life she and Jasper told me of. I try my hardest to remember every detail, but today, her father reminds me of the greatest detail of all. The main reason she left. The main reason she no longer wanted a relationship with him.

It wasn't because of his attitude, manipulation, or control. It was because of a dark secret he had continuously tried to keep from her and the rest of the town.

❀ ❀ ❀

Earlier that day

My sneakers squeak underneath my feet as I turn the corner and head down the long hallway. The hospital is oddly warm and bright, the sun lurking through every open window. It's almost inviting.

Then, why do I feel like throwing up? Why does seeing her father bother me so much? He is just a person. An evil person at that, but he honestly scares me. Both Abernathys do.

With the black and white notebook tightly tucked under my arm, I'm determined to finish the story. Even if Lillian doesn't come to realize what type of life she will live, if she leaves with her father, at least I tried. I tried for Jasper's sake.

I walk past the nurse's station and find myself at a standstill with James. He quickly shuts the door to Lillian's room and gives me a blank stare. "She's resting. Come back later," he states.

I shake my head. "Fine. I'll just sit here and wait for her to wake up then."

I don't believe him. I never believe a word he says. Even if she asked him to step out so she can rest, maybe she's tired of him.

I lean back against the far wall, sliding down to the cold tiled floor. I lay my notebook over my lap and cross my arms, my eyes still locked on the man.

He scoffs before laughing. He searches the walls as he throws his hands onto his hips. "Connor, don't be dramatic. She might sleep for the rest of the day. Come back later, or I'll call you when she wakes up."

"I doubt that."

His shiny black suit shoes inch toward me. "Connor, you have to stop this. Stop being dramatic. She's coming home with me whether you like it or not. End of story. Everything is okay now."

"You're only saying that because her memory is wiped."

He paces in a circle and smiles, stopping to look at me. He itches his chin. "Of course I am. She doesn't remember one horrible thing that I've done or said. It's a new start for me. I can finally make it right."

"Like how you used your words to break her? To belittle her? Trying not be a narcissist this time?"

His smile quickly turns into a frown. "Something like that," he snarls. "It'll be a fresh start. Just let me enjoy it with my daughter. She deserves it."

"She deserves a loving family. Not whatever you are trying to be. You honestly don't think she won't recognize the man behind the mask? The man you're pretending to be? The man you always have been and never will be anything else?"

"One can hope," he says. "Like I said, she doesn't remember a damn thing I said or have done. So, it's a win-win in my eyes."

I grow tired of arguing and stay silent. The more I stare down at the polished tiles, the more my mind questions him. He keeps mentioning how proud he will be that she doesn't remember anything. That can't be a coincidence, can it?

"What's so damn important about Lillian's memory loss anyway? It can't be just so you can get it good with the Taylors again. What are you holding back, James?" I challenge him. "Need help to get votes to be elected mayor again? Your daughter being in a frightening accident will help tug at the hearts of your voters… But we both know that's not it, either, is it?"

His left eye twitches at the mention of his first name. He knows I'm tired of being nice and respectful, that I'm bold enough to call him by his first name, but also that I achieved my goal. I got under his skin. I have his heart pumping in the palm of my hand, and he's scared. He doesn't like it, and I'm on to him. His jaw relaxes. "I think it's time for you to go now. As I said, she's resting. Don't make me take you off the visitors' list."

I slightly laugh, pushing myself off the floor. "I'll be back," I warn. "I'm going to finish my story. Even if she doesn't remember by the end, at least I tried."

"Whatever makes you happy, kid."

❀ ❀ ❀

I find myself at the mercy of Jasper's bedside. With my head in my hands and my elbows resting on my knees, I feel defeated. "I don't know what else to do," I say. "She's not remembering. Nothing is triggering her memories."

"There's nothing you can do," Anna says. Her hand rubs my back. "It just takes time. It takes time for her memories to come back. Her mind needs time to heal. Like it takes time for Jasper to wake."

"I hate this. Greyson doesn't deserve this. He's been through enough already," I sniffle. I wipe my nose on the back of my hand and shake my head. My view toward his body.

"Greyson will be fine. He's a strong little boy. You know that." Her voice is soothing and smooth. "Why don't you get some rest? Quit trying to fix things that can't be fixed. You can't force two puzzle pieces together. Sometimes they just don't fit right."

I nod in agreement. I sit up and straighten out my back against the hard chair. The more I think about the situation, the more I realize what's coming next. "If Jasper won't make her remember, the next part of the story will."

Her long eyelashes bat themselves at me. Anna's mind begins to file back to the specific memory, and by the time she remembers, her mouth parts slightly. "You can't tell her that," she gasps. "That'll destroy her soul all over again."

"She needs to know. The secret is bound to come out all over again anyway. It always does," I urge. "Her father always manages to tell on himself."

"So, you let him do it then."

"But if I do, then she leaves with him and falls back into his old ways. She can't go back to that life. Jasper wouldn't have it. It has to be now, so she can make up her mind before she's released."

She sighs, crossing her arms against her chest as she crosses her legs. "Damn bastard. I can't believe he got away with it."

I sigh, pushing myself up from the chair. "Do you want a cup of coffee? I'm going to run down to the cafeteria to grab something to snack on."

She smiles lightly. "Yeah, I'll take a cup. Thanks."

Then

Lillian

My mind is numb from the information that has been laid out before me. I don't know what to do with it or how to handle it. My soul has disappeared from my body and is lost in a sea of darkness. I don't question my father. I don't want to know the details. My father is a bad person, but he isn't a liar. He's never lied to me. He's hidden things from me and just won't tell me stuff, but he doesn't lie or make excuses. My father has always been straightforward.

It was shocking to hear that my mother loved another man. I always thought my parents' love was genuine. And even though my father didn't change into a selfish prick until the night she died, he was always someone who worked hard for his family's happiness. Maybe I was wrong. Maybe they had issues in their relationship that they hid away from me. Doesn't every relationship have issues, though? Maybe everything I know about my parents is all wrong. Maybe he was a selfish prick even then, and that's what sent my mother into another man's arms.

Part of me feels hurt, but the other half is almost grateful for his honesty.

I sit up from staring at the ceiling, grabbing my purse from the other side of the bed and throwing the strap over my shoulder. I rip my jacket from the foot of the bed, hanging it over my arm. Mentally, I'm not ready to go to school, but I know it has to be done if I want to graduate on time.

A week has flown by since I last saw Jasper, and honestly, it seems like it's been forever. We've talked every day on the phone since our first date, and we plan to go out again tonight. He's been trying his hardest to help me through my family's drama, but I don't think he even understands it.

Bless his heart. I barely speak about anything else.

"It's just a hard pill to swallow," I mumble with the phone pressed between my ear and my shoulder as I walk over to the large mirror. I smooth out my school skirt and sigh. The dark circles under my eyes are noticeable now. "The shopping bags had two watches in them! Two! How can I be so stupid? The secret was right in front of me that day, and I didn't even notice. I just thought they were both for my father!"

"Lillian, breathe, darlin'."

"And another thing—"

He cuts me off and changes the subject. "Will I see you tonight?"

"You'll see me in like ten minutes." I grin. "My father is going to drop me off to get my car."

"Ten minutes? You didn't think to give me a warning? I could have dressed better."

I laugh. "What are you trying to tell me? That you don't smell good all the time?"

"Well, I mean, I have deodorant on."

I snort, still looking at myself in the mirror. "That's good enough. You're overthinking it, Jasper."

"Just trying to make a good impression, Lillian."

I hear footsteps creeping down the hallway outside of my door, and I quickly go into liar mode. "Alright, Brad, I'll see you at school. I shouldn't be too late," my voice changes into a more serious tone now. "Yeah, tell your parents I said 'hello.'"

"Your daddy is right there, isn't he?"

"Mhmm."

He sighs, "Alright, darlin'. I'll let you go. I'll see you soon."

The line clicks.

My father knocks on the door before slowly opening it. He barely peeks inside, but I can tell he's been crying. This is the first time I've seen him in the past week. He has tried his best to avoid me and has rarely said two words to me.

I raise an eyebrow, waiting for him to speak.

"All ready for school?"

This is the first time he's asked me that in two years. I wake myself and drive myself to school every day. I usually text him when I arrive at school or yell through the house to let him know that I'm leaving. But in the last two years, he hasn't made sure that I'm awake and ready.

I take a deep breath. "Yup. I, uh... Do you mind driving me by the Smith's shop?"

His nose wrinkles fowl. "Lillian, what did we just have this discussion about?"

I throw my hands up in defense. "I know. I know. My car is there, remember? He should finish it today, so you don't have to worry about having your assistant drive me to school."

He lets out a deep sigh and rubs the back of his neck. "Yeah, that's fine. I'll drop you off on my way into the office."

138

I follow him down the hall and down the stairs. He grabs his keys from the hook on the wall, continuing to lead me out the door to his truck. "Was that Brad on the phone that I heard you talking to?" he asks, as he climbs behind the wheel.

My body sinks into the leather seat as I relax. I slam the door shut behind me and quickly buckle in. "Yeah," I lied.

"Hm. Make sure he comes by sometime soon. It's been a while since I've seen him or his parents. Maybe we should invite them to Thanksgiving?"

"Are we actually doing Thanksgiving this year? We never do Thanksgiving anymore."

He pulls out of the driveway and speeds down the main road. "Well, maybe we should? You know, as a family."

His words baffle me. What happened to my father, and who is this man? We don't do holidays. We haven't since my mother died. It's just not something we do. We aren't a family anymore. We're barely father and daughter.

"Uh, if you want?" I stare out the window. My mind races as I find the proper words to speak my mind. I guess this is going to be a weird morning because I also have some words that I never thought I would say. "Thank you for keeping that a secret. I'm sorry I pushed you to your breaking point of telling me the truth."

For the past week, it's been eating me alive. I've wanted to say thank you for sheltering me from the truth, but I could never find the right words to say. That or he hasn't been around to tell him what's been on my mind.

We come close to a stop sign, and he slams on the brakes. He taps on the steering wheel with his thumbs, almost playing a tune. He stays silent as he thinks for a moment, but then he finally says, "I didn't want the image of your mother to be tampered with. I did love your mother, but even after all this time, I'm still angry. She died, and it left me with no resolution. Questions were left unanswered. I didn't want you to be left with the same outcome."

For the first time in my life, I almost feel bad for my father. "Who was the other man?" I realize as the words roll off my tongue that I quickly want to swallow them back. I'm not sure I'm ready for the answers that he has, but I can't help but feel curious. "Did she ever tell you?"

He straightens his back and doesn't look at me. His eyes search the empty road as we just sit at the empty crossroads. "I, uh…" He almost begins to cry. His voice breaks a little. "No, I never found out. As I said, there are so many questions that she never answered. I often wonder if her death was even an accident."

"What do you mean by that?" I bite my lip, confused.

"Maybe all the guilt ate her up, and she killed herself."

My breath is whisked away, surprised he would even think that she would kill herself for the sake of a secret affair coming to light. "She wouldn't," I gasp. "That's not her. She wouldn't leave us like that."

A horn behind us blares.

He rolls his eyes, and a frown is forced onto his face. Anger replaces the depressed man that has been moping around for the past week, and I can feel his aura radiating off him. "Why are you sticking up for her? You don't know the type of woman she was. She cheated on me, remember? So, what makes you think she wouldn't do something else idiotic like kill herself and make it look like an accident?"

There he is. My father has returned.

The horn blares again followed by a woman's firm tone.

Instead of finally driving through the stop sign, he rolls down the window and begins a very unfriendly argument with the woman behind him. As he frantically screams at her, my anxiety increases.

It pisses me off that he uses his title to get away with everything, especially when he uses the Taylors as his backup leverage. Almost as a get-out-of-trouble card. They have bailed him out of almost everything possible, and I'm slightly concerned for his career. I wouldn't doubt if they were close to impeaching him. That or I'm almost guaranteed that no one will vote for him again once his four years as mayor expire. Unless Mr. Taylor buys the votes again or tampers with the numbers.

I grab my purse and get out of the truck, slamming the door.

"Hey!" My father's head spins toward me. "Where the hell do you think you are going?"

"I'm walking to Jasper's shop."

"No—" Before he can finish yelling at me, I stop him. I lean forward and rest my arm on the window.

"You are making a fool of yourself. Do you know that? Go to work, or go back home. I really don't care, but this is insane. You are not in the right state of mind to be in public." I gestured to the old woman, who was now out of her car. "Look at yourself! You are screaming at an old woman because she honked her horn at you!"

"I don't care what the crusty old bit—"

141

"There you go again!" I shut him down once more. "Go home! I'm tired of your bullshit, and I'm tired of you. I'm done with everything."

"Lillian," he growls. "Watch your mouth, and get back in the fucking truck."

"No," I challenge. "Like I said, I am done. I'm done with you. With this lifestyle. I'm done. I'd rather be dead with my mother than spend one more second with you."

"You selfish bitch," he spits through his gritted teeth. "You are going to ruin this for us, and I'm not going to stand by and watch it happen. Hell is going to rain, little girl. Mark my words."

I don't want to have a relationship with my father. Who wants that? I had the best relationship with him before he became vile and twisted. I want nothing more than to have things go back to the way they were, but it's gotten to the point where it's crossed a line. And it can never go back to the way things were.

My lips curl into a smirk, pushing myself off the side of the truck. I look both ways before crossing the empty road and don't look back. His truck revs up behind me. The man is trying to frighten me. He's angry and tired of his misfortune. He's defeated.

As I continue down the road, I hear his truck tires squeal as they take off down the road in a different direction. Luckily, we'd made it close to Jasper's shop, so it isn't that far of a walk, and I don't mind the cold. My blood had been boiling all morning, and the cold almost feels good against my skin.

The diner and the shop come into view. Both buildings are slightly busy, and their parking lots are almost full.

I race down the hill to Jasper's shop. The cold cuts through my face, and my nose stings, my eyes watering as my teeth chatter.

Jasper steps outside through the bay doors, paperwork in one hand as he speaks to a customer on the phone. His body is tightly snug with a gray button-up sweater, his cheeks flushed from the cold. His blue eyes dart in my direction, and his face falls.

The phone drops from his ear. "Lillian, did you walk here?"

I quickly drop my bag from my shoulder and throw my arms around his neck, smashing my lips onto his. His lips are just as cold, but they're soft and dance perfectly with mine.

His body abruptly falls back, but he finds his footing quickly and deepens the kiss. The office phone and paperwork are let go, falling out of his grip. He wraps his arms around my waist, holding me tightly against his body. "Lillian," he moans into my lips.

I slightly pull away, catching my breath. I bite my bottom lip and fight every urge to keep from kissing this man. I had a taste, and I'm hungry for more.

By the look on his face, he must sense that I want more and leans forward, pecking my lips a few times before asking, "Where is your father? I thought he was bringing you to the shop today." He sets me down but still keeps his arms intact around my body.

"I ditched him and decided to walk," I shrug. "He was acting like an ass. No more than usual. I'm just tired of it."

His hand reaches up and brushes a few strands of hair behind my ear. His palm caresses my cheek, and his thumb circles slowly. "Lillian, don't make me sound like a broken record. You know how I feel about the whole situation. Especially now that he knows about me."

I smile. "No, Jasper. I choose you. I choose you and everything that life has to offer me. I told my father that I was done with everything and that I never want to go back to the life that he wants me to live."

His pearly whites make an appearance as his pink lips stretch into a smile. "Really?"

"Really," I nod, as I lay my forehead against his. I let out a deep sigh and close my eyes for a second. Everything that was once attached and weighing down my body is gone. I feel free. "I'm sorry it took me so long to stand up to him, but I'm glad you pushed me to be the person I needed to be."

He shakes his head and kisses my forehead. "Why are you apologizing? Don't apologize—"

"I usually don't," I half laugh.

"Then, don't apologize for this. You stood up to him. You stood up to him on your terms and when you met your limit, and I am so proud of you for that."

Butterflies flutter in my stomach. That's all I ever wanted from someone. Besides love and acceptance, I wanted someone to be proud of me.

"I want to take you somewhere." His hand drops to my shoulder, and I almost wish that I wasn't wearing this sweater. I crave his touch.

"Where?"

"Meet me here after school, and I'll show you." He pecks my lips before slipping away, snatching the scattered paperwork and office phone from the ground. He takes a moment and puts the papers back in order.

I lick my lips, puzzled. I narrow my eyes and throw my hip out to the side. "School? You don't want to spend the day together?"

He looks up. "Darlin', believe me. I want to spend every breathtaking moment with you. But I'm not going to let you drop out of school or let you fail all because you don't want to leave me. That's just silly, and you'll have no future like that. I want to see you succeed, not be a bum like me."

Even though I hate the thought of leaving him, I agree. I have one more year of high school, and I can't just throw that away. After thirteen years of school, I'm almost finished. Then, if I decide to go to college, that can be on my terms, but for right now, I need to finish what I started.

Now

Lillian

Connor's entire demeanor suddenly changes. The room falls silent, but the air is heavy and thick. It feels suffocating, and I don't understand it.

He closes the notebook and plops it onto the ground beside him. He leans forward with his hands intertwined, his elbows resting on his knees. His eyes avoid mine, and he bounces his knee.

"What's wrong?" I cock my head to the side and reach out to touch him. He sits back up and moves his hands away from me. "I don't understand. Did I do something wrong? Why did you stop reading? I was enjoying it so much."

"Did your father tell you that I came by to see you yesterday?" he finally says, still not looking at me.

I think back to yesterday. Besides the casualness of just laying in bed, I snuck out to see Jasper a few times in the middle of the night. His mother warmly greeted me once, but the next few times, she was fast asleep next to him in a chair. My father visited me once, but then quickly scrambled out the door. He promised to return but didn't.

At the very least, I was fortunate that my father brought real clothes. Warm fuzzy socks and pajamas. I was tired of wearing blue gowns that let my back hang out.

I sit up and slip a leg underneath my bottom, throwing the other leg off the side of the bed. I suck my bottom lip in. "What? No?"

"Figures," he scoffs. He almost hesitates, like he wants to say more, but he keeps it to himself and stays quiet.

"I was hoping you were going to show. I was pretty bored yesterday."

"I'm sorry," he says, as he finally meets my gaze. "I tried to see you. I did."

I smile lightly. "Is that all that's bothering you? Is that why you stopped reading?"

He shoves his hair off his forehead and sighs. "No. I-I, um, Lillian, this part of your story is tough. It's the main reason you wanted nothing to do with your father."

"But I thought it was because of the fight we had? The way he acted after he told me about my mother's affair?"

His eyes flutter, and you can almost hear his heart crack. "Uh, no, Lil. It wasn't because of that. That was the beginning, but it gets worse."

My smile fades, and all I can do is stare at my best friend. I don't want to believe him, but I know he isn't lying. He has no reason to lie. It doesn't benefit him.

Without hesitation, I blurt out, "Tell me."

"Lillian, it's not that simple."

"No, tell me, Connor. I can handle it."

"Lillian, I really don't think—"

"Dammit, Connor!" I cut him off. "Tell me. I'm leaving with that monster in less than twenty-four hours. Now, give me a reason to not try to fix the issues I have against him. Because part of me is hoping he has changed within the last two years with me not being in his life, but the other half of me is screaming to not believe a single word he has to say." My chest is rising and falling at this point, angry and frustrated. "Do you think I should leave with him tomorrow and give him another chance?"

"No."

My hand stretches out and circles in the air. "Then, tell me what the hell happened before I leave without knowing the truth. Because God knows, he won't ever fucking tell me."

"Fine…" As the words pour out of Connor's mouth, he quickly realizes that he didn't warn me for the gut-wrenching part. The truth. It might be unbearable, but I need to hear it.

I sit silently staring at my fuzzy pink socks, chewing on the side of my cheek. I blink and a tear drops onto my cheek. The new information tries its best to soak in, but my heart doesn't want to accept it. "That's why I never spoke to him again," I whisper.

"Lil…" He reaches for my hand, but I coil them into my chest, as my heart pounds against them, my arms rattling. "Tell me, why did he do it? Tell me why he isn't in fucking prison right now for what he did."

He gulps and chokes on his words. His blue eyes gloss over.

"Tell me, Connor. Don't fucking stop there."

Before he can answer, we hear a knock at the door. Brad's head wraps around the corner and then he eventually pushes it open all the way, entering the room with a smile on his face. Once he realizes that I am crying, he is swiftly at my side. "What happened? What's wrong?"

I don't know whether to cry, throw up, or fling something. So many emotions run amuck. "Did you know?" I ask quietly.

"Did I know what?"

"Did you know about the power that my father holds?" my voice cracks, but I'm louder now. "Did you know?"

Brad doesn't know whether to be confused or excited. His dark eyes peer down at me. "Did you get your memory back?"

"No." I lay back against the pile of pillows against my headboard. "Connor just told me some interesting intel about my father."

He runs a hand through his messy hair, nervous. "Connor," he barks. "What the hell, man?"

I lean forward, "No. You leave him out of it. He is the only person who has the guts to tell me the truth. You and my father have been tiptoeing around these secrets and keeping them from me ever since I woke up!"

Brad stops in his tracks, glaring at Connor. "The whole truth? Like everything?"

I could sense that they were feeling each other out. The tone in his voice is almost questionable and less hostile. He's softening up. Connor blinks for a moment and then shakes his head. He looks down at the ground. "Well, the secret. I didn't tell her everything."

"There's more?" My head spins between them.

Connor grows quiet. "Your father had Brad burn down Jasper's father's shop."

Before I can interject, Brad's voice leaps from his chest, "Hey! What the hell, Harris?"

I feel numb. I'm tired of fighting and, frankly, crying over the past, but still... I don't know if I could handle any more news.

"She has the right to know, Taylor!" Connor rises to his feet.

"Enough!"

Connor sits back down.

"Lillian, I was young and stupid. I didn't realize the damage I caused until after I watched that building go up in flames." Brad sighs, grabbing the doctor's rolling stool from the corner of the room and pulling it to my bedside. He fidgets with his hair and looks at Connor, nervous still. "I'm sorry."

"Sorry? Did you apologize to Jasper and his mother?" I ask sharply. "Why did you think it was a good idea to listen to my father?"

"It wasn't just him. My parents ordered me to do it, too."

I roll my eyes, crossing my arms. My nose sniffles, and I shake my head in disappointment. It isn't anything new. It's the same bullshit that I always knew him for.

"Lillian, I found out everything the same night you did, which led me to have a full fight with my parents and then eventually led me to leave. After learning everything that night, I finally understood everything through your eyes... I made a life of my own and refused to come back to this fucking town."

"Why did you then?" I ask. "Why did you come back?"

"For you. I... No matter how much shit that happened between us, I had to come back for you. Your father rang me up. I didn't believe him at first, but then I knew I had to come back to save you. To save you from him. He is already trying to make deals with my parents again. To use not only you but me for his selfish reasons. I moved on a year ago. I knew you were happy with Jasper, and I knew I couldn't compete with that. Or ever get your forgiveness to be able to just be friends, so I left you alone. I left you to live your life."

"Then, why are you here?" Connor asks, earning a glare from Brad before he turns back to me.

"I genuinely have feelings for you, Lil. After that night, I felt closer to you than I ever have before. I thought I could fix things between us this past week…"

"For your selfish reasons?"

He nods. "For my selfish reasons."

I pull my legs to my chest, my head pounding from exhaustion. I need to hear everything they had to offer. I'm surprised that nothing has triggered my memories. It would save me the heartbreak all over again.

"Alright, tell me. Tell me what happened that night. I want to know every gruesome detail. Don't leave a damn part out." My finger points between the both of them. "No more secrets. I can't handle it anymore. So, if you have anything else you would like to tell me, tell me now."

Connor throws his hands up. "That's everything from me."

"And I'm about to help finish the rest of the story for you right now," Brad adds.

"Go for it," I utter. "I'm ready whenever you are. I have nowhere else to be."

Then

Lillian

The last bell rang. I quickly slip out the door and into the now crowded hall, making a beeline for my locker. I do my best to not be social at the end of the day and make excuses for everything. One girl from my cheerleading squad asked me if I wanted to attend a party later tonight. Usually, I would accept and attend it with Brad. She looked horrified when I denied it. Like the audacity of my denial, she didn't like it.

I drop my book bag to my feet and dig out my textbooks, shoving them neatly into my locker. My eyes flicker to the awkward pictures of Brad and me that I have taped to the inside of my locker door. My stomach turns as I stare at the pathetic fake smile I wear on my face.

I remember that day so vividly. It was one of the very first weeks we started dating. I wasn't sure of the whole situation yet, but I wanted to try my hardest to understand. Anything for my father. Right before he lost his marbles.

I pull down the pictures and crumble them beneath my fist, chunking them over my shoulder. I don't need them. It's a constant reminder of the life that I refuse to go back to. The life I never understood but was forced into for money.

"What the hell, Lillian?" a voice says from behind me.

I turn and lean against the neighbor's locker. I watch as Brad unfolds the pictures in his hands, and he looks livid. "What are you doing?" he questions, waving the pictures in the air. "Why are you getting rid of these?"

"Because we aren't a thing."

"Listen, I know you're like super pissed at me. But come on. You're overreacting," he coos, as he inches forward. "We aren't over. We can't be. You promised you would try, too. You've been avoiding me all week. You have answered none of my calls or texts... I didn't think you would be this pissed at me for being rude to you the last time we spoke. I understand you didn't want to have dinner with my parents, okay? And I'm sorry that I was a little bitch, but you don't have to give me the silent treatment."

I squint my eyes and cock my head to the side. "You think this is about—" I shut my eyes and take a few deep breaths before opening them, then fake a smile. "This isn't about that conversation. It's about how rude you are regardless of any conversation we have, Brad. It's not healthy. We are not healthy. I've concluded that I want no more toxicity in my life."

His teeth graze his bottom lip, his chest rumbling from a small chuckle rising from within. "You're seriously ending things? With me? You know what's going to happen, right? You are breaking part of the agreement. Your father will lose everything," he warns.

I turn back to my locker and shut the door. I grab my bag off the floor, throwing it onto my back. "Yeah, I already had this talk with my father. Thanks. We can move on from the subject already. I'll tell you what I told him. I really don't care."

"You're really doing this?"

"You sound surprised," I snort, as I push past him. My hand snakes to my bookbag strap, and I clench the rough material. He follows, pushing people out of the way to keep at my side. "This is because of him, isn't it?" He pushes in front of me and stops me in my tracks.

"Who?" I play dumb.

He rolls his eyes. "Oh, come on, Lillian. It's the talk of the town! The guy you've been sneaking around for everyone to see. The one that owns that shop on the other side of town. Tony and Son's, is it? What is so special about him? What did he do? Did he put these fairytales into your head? Did he promise you the world? Oh, I bet he promised you a better life, too."

"Stop."

He circles me. "All these promises and false hopes. Why? So, he can get you naked?"

"Don't talk about him that way. You don't know him like I do."

"Like you do? Lillian, if I know anything about men, it is that they will tell you anything to get you to sleep with them."

My hand balls into a fist at my side as the words rattle inside my head. He's stupid, manipulative, and immature. It infuriates me.

Everyone is staring now, and the once abrupt and excited hallway fades. Everyone loves a good fight. "Shut. Up. Brad."

"Oh. My. God," he covers his mouth, mocking me. He's enjoying this. "Tell me you haven't already slept with him, Lillian."

I stay silent. My eyes cut into him like daggers.

He grabs my shoulders, shaking me. "I bet you already have. I bet he's already touched every inch of you. He's probably already told his friends all about the looks of you, too. How you caved in willingly because you think he has such desires for you. Probably even love—"

"And? What if I have?" I'm in his face now, challenging him. "Don't be upset that you've never had the privilege of undressing me. To know what it's like when I scream out your name. To know how I taste."

Brad throws his head back and laughs. He runs both hands through his dark hair, yanking frustratedly. He puts his hands on his hip, marching in a circle as he stares at the ceiling. His jaw is clenched. His face is flushed, and he lunges forward toward the locker. He punches it, denting it slightly.

I ignore everyone's whispers as I inch toward him and grab his now crippled hand. The knuckles are bleeding, but he doesn't resist my touch. I hold his hand in both of mine, and my thumb rubs circles into his warm skin. I gulp and look up at him, his eyes wild. I lick my lips. "I hope one day you find your freedom in all of this. To leave this town and find Rileigh. To tell her everything you have ever wanted to tell her, and if she has already moved on, then I hope you find someone who will love you unconditionally the way that I can never love you."

He stays silent, and his eyes fall to the floor. I kiss his cheek and drop his hand, backing away slowly and leaving the hallway. I follow the crowd of kids out of the school and into the parking lot, finding my car quickly.

As promised, I return to Jasper. He waits anxiously outside of his mechanic shop, wiping his hands on a dirty rag. I throw my car into park and fling the door open, jumping out of my punch bug. I run to him and throw my hands around his neck, burying my face in his chest.

The smell of a weird variety fills my nose. Oil, some dirt, and strong cologne. It reminds me that things are often desired when it's worked for and not handed to you.

He squeezes me tight as he wraps his muscular arms around me. He nuzzles his face into my shoulder, sighing heavily. "That bad of a day, huh?" he mumbles into my hair.

I can't speak. I begin to choke up as the tears flow down my face. The feeling of being flustered is something I hate. That every conversation has to be a fight with no resolution.

Brad and I never really had a civil relationship. Even before we started dating, he was still the same alpha male meathead that everyone loves and hates.

I want nothing more than for him to find his peace of mind, to find a place in this world where he isn't poked or yanked apart. I can't say that he never meant something to me because I spent almost every waking moment with him for the last two years. I just never loved the kid.

"It's over now," he reassures. "I know you probably don't want to talk about it, but I'm here for you. Whenever you are ready to vent. Your feelings are valid."

My feelings are valid.

Butterflies swarm my stomach as the air is lifted through my chest, and I feel like I'm floating away. A voice inside screams that this isn't true. It's a dream. A dream where someone cares about you. It can't be real, and it shouldn't be real. *You're going to hell, Lillian. For all the shit you say and do. You've turned sour in the last two years, and no one wants to be your friend, let alone near you. You don't deserve someone like Jasper. Why would someone like him want to be around someone like you?*

But my feelings are valid.

If he wanted something from you, he would have already taken it like every other selfish prick—

Stop!

I push him away softly. "Damn you." I cover my face as my eyes pour.

"Did I do something wrong? Was it something I said?"

I nod and pull my hands away from my face. His mouth falls slightly, and he tries to reach out, "Lillian—"

I take a step back. "I don't understand what you are doing to me! Never have I ever started to have self-doubts about myself. I'm questioning my every thought and my every action with you. If this thing between us is even real or some made-up fantasy in my head to escape the fucked up life I'm living in. You have my head spinning and my heart pounding," I continue. "These things don't happen to me. They don't. I'm falling way too hard, and I'm way in too deep, Jasper."

"Lillian, you're freaking out, darlin'." His voice is soft.

"Why? Why am I freaking out?"

"You're scared," he steps forward. "You're scared of the feeling of empathy and compassion… acceptance and reassurance… stability and companionship. You're scared, and that's okay because you've never felt this before."

He takes a step forward and grabs my wrist. The warmth of his skin melts me away and turns me into jello as he pulls me into an embrace. His rough hand slides up and outlines my jaw with his finger, pulling my chin closer to his face. He gives me a quick peck, his breath heavy.

"Don't be scared to let someone worship you," he states. "Because you know what? You are enough in someone else's eyes. You are good enough. You are beautiful enough. You are worthy enough. You are strong enough. You are more than enough. And if you can't see that right now, then I'm going to remind you every single day."

This is what I've been missing.

I find it hard to put words together. I'm flustered and heated. I could barely look him in the eye without feeling bashful and shy.

After a few more hours at the shop, the sun burns out, and darkness is the only thing left. The cold is bitter on my skin. I should have packed some kind of clothing before threatening to never go back home again, but I didn't plan the day out like this.

Jasper turns off every light in the barn, shutting the bay doors behind him and locking them up tight with a padlock and chain. I anxiously waited for him to finish, my knees buckling from the wind. I hold my arms tight around my scrawny body. My light sweater that the school usually makes us wear is not very warm. It's scratchy, and it often irritates my skin.

"Where are you taking me tonight?" I ask, my teeth chattering. You can almost see the heat of my breath.

He throws his shop keys into his pocket and snakes an arm around my waist, turning me around. We walk past his truck and to the edge of the road. He nods toward the diner across the street.

"I was going to take you far out in the country, but I heard it's supposed to rain a little later, and I don't feel like getting stuck on some back road in the mud," he chuckles. "But then I got to thinking… you've never really had fun before. Like just cut loose and not have a single thought in your mind."

His accent is thick. "I went over to Big Mama's Tasty Treat this morning for some coffee, and they are throwing a little holiday party tonight. Adults only, of course. Only if you want to, though."

My teeth chatter some more as I shiver. "Anything that keeps us out of the cold, but it sounds fun. I just hope they don't remember me. I was not a part of the mass destruction that Brad and his friends caused."

He chuckles and walks me across the street, his arm still wrapped around me. We weave through the cars that are parked and find ourselves inside.

My skin stings as it thaws out. The heat feels amazing. I hate the cold and always wanted to move somewhere hot.

I rub my hands together as my eyes scan the busy restaurant. Almost every seat is taken. The music and chatter fill the room along with the glorious smell of food. Homemade paper snowflakes hang from the ceiling tiles, illuminated by twinkling Christmas lights on every wall and tucked into every corner.

Everyone is playing various board games, and a few groups are getting rowdy.

I turn into Jasper, "It's not even Thanksgiving yet?" I casually point to the Christmas tree in the back corner.

He leans down, and his lips brush my ear. "Yeah, but the holidays are the best time of the year."

I turn back around and watch as an elderly woman strolls up to the counter. "Just two tonight, Jasper?" she asks, collecting menus from next to the cash register.

"Yes, ma'am."

Her gray wrinkly eyes fall upon me. Her tiny red lips form almost a smirk. "I hope you aren't back to cause more trouble, missy. It took me days to clean the place. They plastered food all over the walls and ceiling," she complains.

My heart drops to my feet. I should have stayed behind and helped, but I didn't.

"I'm so sorry." I shake my head. "I swear, I had no idea that they would behave like that. I knew they could act like children, but I didn't realize they did stupid shi… stuff like that. They have no respect for anything or anyone."

Her eyes rise to look at Jasper. "Well, it looks like you finally found someone who isn't so childish. Jasper is a good boy. He is something extraordinary. He always has been since he was a boy," she beams. It's almost as if she's replaying all the memories she has with Jasper in her head, even if it was just a slight encounter. She blinks and snaps out of it. "Right this way. We have a seat for you in the back."

She motions to follow her with the flick of her finger, shuffling across the checkerboard floor. She leads us toward the back of the room, often stopping for a moment as she comments on someone's game.

As we slide into the booth, she sets the menus down in front of us on the cold table. She licks her lips, then grabs a notebook from her back pocket and slides a pencil out from behind her ear. "Your waitress might be a moment. From the way that it's looking from here, she might be losing in a game of poker. So, for right now, I'll be grabbing your drinks. What will you be having? The usual, Jasper?"

He leans back against the red cushioning. His hands fiddle with the menu, flipping through it. "Not tonight," he gives a small smile. "I don't need coffee at this hour of the night. It'll keep me up. My son wakes me up too damn early, so there's no point in trying to sleep in."

"How is that rascal? It's been a while since you've brought him in here."

"I've been too busy at the shop, Big Mama. Sometime this weekend, I will bring him. I promise," he swears.

This is Big Mama? She isn't big at all. A scrawny little old lady. She's as tall as me when I'm sitting down. My mind races with so many questions, but I don't dare open my mouth to ask them.

"I'll take a hot chocolate," Jasper chimes. He turns his head in my direction. "What about you, darlin'? What are you hankering for?"

Be adventurous, Lillian.

"I think I will have the same thing. Thanks."

She nods and shuffles away, quickly finding herself lost in a conversation not very far away from our table.

I shiver with excitement and lean forward. "Hot chocolate? What are we? Five?"

He leans forward, intertwining his finger on the table's surface. "Listen, you didn't have to order the same thing that I ordered. You're a big girl. You can make your own decisions."

I laugh at his witty comment. "I just thought that I would try something new tonight."

"New? What do you mean 'new?'" He raises an eyebrow. The menu slides out of his hands and flops onto the table, his mouth ajar. "Lillian Grace Abernathy, are you telling me that you've never had hot chocolate before?" he asks, almost amazed. "What kind of world are you living in?"

161

I grab the menu, turning its pages. "A shitty one, apparently."

After a few laughs and a quick look at the menu, Big Mama is replaced by our very young waitress. She looks a few years younger than I am but is much taller. Her long face is dotted with cute freckles. Her eyes are a dark brown, her hair straight and blonde.

She sets mugs out in front of us. The hot chocolate steams through the pile of marshmallows and whipped cream. The smell is impeccable.

I squint down at the mug. "Jasper."

Like a giddy kid, he grins down at his mug, cupping it and bringing it up to his lips. As he sips, the whipped cream mixes within his facial hair, forming a very foamy mustache across his upper lip. "It's so good."

"We are literally drinking dessert!" I laugh.

He sets his mug down and looks up at our waitress. "She's never had hot chocolate. Can you believe it?"

The waitress's smile disappears as her eyes shift in my direction. "Wait, seriously?"

"Is it that hard to believe?" I nearly shout. "It's just hot chocolate!"

"Don't sound too good for the hot chocolate, darlin'. Give it a try."

I roll my eyes and give in. My hands cup the fairly large cup and bring it to my lips. The ceramic mug is warm against my skin. "This is ridiculous. This is dessert."

"She must be real fun at parties," the waitress chimes in, leaning closer to Jasper.

"That's her problem," he whispers. "She doesn't know how to have fun."

I lower the cup. "You know I'm sitting right here, right? I can hear you."

Jasper throws his head back and groans, "Lillian. Drink the damn thing already."

I heavily sigh and bring the cup back up to my lips, the chocolaty substance filling my nose. I take a quick sip and find myself smiling as the cold whipped cream tickles my lips. The warm substance fills my belly. "Mmmm."

Jasper claps. "I knew you'd enjoy it!"

I giggle and set my mug down, my tongue wiping away the foam from my lips. I tuck my auburn hair behind my ear and toss it over my shoulder. "It wasn't bad. I'm very impressed."

The waitress clears her throat. "Alright, what can I get y'all?"

I sit up and quickly flip through the menu, trying to decide on what to eat. Everything looks wonderful, and I almost wanted to try a bit of everything, but my eyes are too big for my stomach. "I'm not sure," I say, as I bury my face in the pages.

"How about you, Jasper?" she asks. I hint at a sweetness in the tone of her voice as she says his name.

I look up and watch as she bats her long eyelashes at him, but he doesn't notice as he hands her his menu. He pats away the whipped cream that lingers within his facial hair with a napkin, before saying, "Cassie, will you just bring me a bunch of French toast with bacon, please?"

She nods, tucking the menu underneath her arm. She doesn't bother writing anything down. They trained her mind to remember orders without writing them down. She turns to look at me. Her face becomes sour, but she tries her best to hide it. "And for you?"

I hold the menu out and quickly handed it to her. She looks as if she's going to bite me just for sitting with Jasper. I blink up at her, "I'll have a burger with fries, please?"

She leaves without saying another word, but I can tell she's upset.

I sit back against the cushions, giggling to myself. "You just have a way with women, don't you?"

He raises an eyebrow as he takes another sip from his mug. "What are you talking about?"

"Cassie." I lean forward, grinning.

"What about Cassie?"

"Are you kidding me? She so likes you!"

He chuckles. "I think you're just jealous."

I roll my eyes. "Oh yeah, I'm definitely jealous of a fifteen-year-old."

"She's sixteen and Big Mama's granddaughter."

I snort. "How do you even know that? How often do you come in here?"

He reaches across the table and grabs my hand. "I come in here every morning for a cup of coffee. Around lunchtime, I come back for another cup. I also bring my son here every Sunday for dinner," he shrugs. "So… yeah, I usually don't pop in here that much."

I lightly slap his hand, shaking my head at him. "Funny. You're really funny."

After a few minutes of deciding what board game we should play first, he pulls me out of my seat and dances with me in the aisle. With my hand intertwined in his and a hand on his shoulder, my head lays in the crook of his neck. I object to his madness, afraid of what people will think, but he reassures me that they won't be paying much attention. That they are too wrapped up in playing their games to notice. Plus, I can't say no to a Shania Twain song.

Cassie brings us our plates of dinner after a quick game of Candy Land. I won, and he can't handle the defeat. He begins to throw a small tantrum, throwing his straw wrapper at me and pouting.

"You're lucky we didn't bet anything," I pester him.

His lips form a straight line, his green eyes staring into my soul. "Shut up and eat."

I laugh and dig into my food. A flicker of light catches my eyes, my head turning out of curiosity. With my sleeve, I wipe away the condensation on the inside of the window. The light becomes brighter and larger, the colors illuminating. It almost has a glow to it.

Even with all the cars in the parking lot, I can tell that it's coming from the shop. A thick, sour taste is in my mouth as my stomach churns. "Jasper."

"What?" He shoves the fork into his mouth and packs his cheek full of French toast. His eyes glance up at me and then follow my gaze, as I don't dare to rip them from the flames. He drops his fork onto his plate, rips his jacket from the arm of the chair, and runs up the aisle. He frantically digs into his pocket and throws money onto the counter in front of the cashier and then runs out the door without a single word. "Shit! Shit! Shit!"

I quickly follow. "Call 9-1-1!" I scream, my voice echoing through the now quiet diner.

My arms push against the heavy diner glass door, the bell above ringing as the door opens and slams behind me. I dash across the parking lot and through the maze of cars, stopping at the road as the mechanic's shop comes into full view.

By now, it's too late. We're too late, forced to watch the shop go up in flames. We hear the wooden barn creak, and the wood begins to fall on the inside.

Then

Lillian

Brad and his friends sit on the tailgate of Sam's old pickup truck. They sway their legs as they pop the bottle caps onto the gravel below. They take sips from their beers, laughing.

I make my way across the street, kneeling next to Jasper. He is on his knees with his head in his hands. His cries are loud and gruesome.

I climb to my feet. "What the fuck, Brad?"

"I'm sorry." Brad's smile is mischievous and dark. He hops off the back of the truck, running his fingers through his greasy hair. He wears his football jacket, matching the rest of his friends, and strolls over, cocky and broad. "Your father was worried about you. He sent us to check on you."

"That's bullshit."

"Not bullshit. Didn't he warn you about being with him? Why couldn't you just listen, Lillian? Why couldn't you be a good girl? Why did you have to make me do this? I don't enjoy being the bad guy, Lil! He warned you," he repeats, as his teeth glisten in the light of the flames. "Well, here's your hell now."

I can't see the gold flakes in his eyes, eyes that look solid black. He smells of cigarettes and liquor, his breath hot and sour.

My mind races back to my father's heated argument from earlier. His voice echoes in my mind. *Hell is going to rain.*

Brad watches as my mind puts the pieces together, laughing. "It wasn't long after your little stunt at school that your father found me. Told me all about your lovely morning with him. Well, Lillian, that's just… sad. You're throwing everything away for some dirt poor man. He has no life. Nothing going for him. Nothing to offer you."

I bite my lip, the heat melting away the cold that once lingered in the air. I wince at every word as he sprinkles spit with each one. His hand reaches for the back of my neck, pulling our faces together. His other hand finds itself on my hip. "Did you not just beg me weeks ago to give you more affection?"

I shove him off me. "You're drunk, Brad. This isn't you. You are better than this."

"Answer the question, Lillian. Did you not just ask for more affection within our relationship because you felt I wasn't giving you enough attention?"

"I did, but that was before—"

"Before what? Because how I see it is, you couldn't wait to let me treat you how you deserve to be treated. You find a low life, who is thirsty for pussy—"

"It isn't like that!"

"You cheated on him, honey. You're just mad that you got caught. Just own up to it," Sam eggs on.

Before I can object to anything further, a hand touches my shoulder. My head whips around to find Jasper. His eyes are bloodshot from crying, his cheeks a shade of pink, the fire reflecting in his eyes. "Leave her alone. She doesn't want you anymore."

"Oh, he finally speaks! I was afraid you were going to just cower the whole time and let Lillian fight your battles for you."

Separating Brad and me, Jasper pulls me back and steps in front of me. His arm is still wrapped around my body, pressing me closely behind him. Brad is a few inches taller than Jasper, but both are equally beefy.

"Leave," Jasper repeats. "Now. Get out of here."

"We can't leave just yet," Brad nearly yells. He backs away with his arms stretched out wide. "The show hasn't begun!"

"What show?" I almost whisper. I watch as Brad bounces onto the back of the truck, grabbing his beer and chugging it. He throws it into the fire, and the glass shatters. "What is he talking about?"

Brad howls, cupping his mouth. "Here he comes now!"

A truck's horn blares from down the road. My head darts in its direction as we watch it fly from over the hill and around the corner, sliding into the gravel and coming to a complete stop. The headlights shine directly on us like a spotlight. My father is behind the wheel.

I put my hand up, shielding the light from my eyes. I glance up at Jasper and he stands his ground, his eyes squinting into the light. "Well, looks like I'm finally going to meet your father, darlin'."

He pushes the door open with his foot and jumps out, dropping a bottle of liquor to the ground. He digs in his pocket and pulls out a revolver. It's tiny, but fits perfectly within his hand. He's had that pistol for as long as I can remember. He hides it in a safe inside his study, hidden in the wall behind a fancy family portrait.

169

I grip tightly the back of Jasper's sweater and press my cheek against his back. "Yeah, never a better time than right now." I gulp, terrified of his next move. I've never seen such evil radiate from my father before. This isn't him, and a part of me feels guilty. Did I do this to him? Did I make him into the monster that stands before me? What if I never stood my ground and let him continue to live my life for me? Would he have been different?

His hand holding the gun shakes. He's drunk and out of his mind. His silver hair is a mess, and his suit isn't put together right. His tie hangs loose around his neck, his shirt hangs halfway tucked out of his pants. He's not even wearing two of the same shoes.

"Where are the damn police?" I mumble under my breath.

But he must have heard me. "Do you think that I don't have control over this town? This is my mother fucking town, Lillian! I am the mayor for crying out loud, and I might have bought some time from them, sweetie. You know, to look the other way until I am finished with your boyfriend." He stumbles as he walks, but manages to get closer, burping.

"Why are you doing this? Why is it so hard for you to let me go? Let me live my own life." My voice is timid and quiet, shaking as I watch him come unraveled.

He shrugs. "You know the answer to that. You are a part of the packaged deal. If I don't deliver, then I don't get paid."

"Why is there a deal in the first place? We don't live in the Stone Age where you marry off your daughter for money or a cow," Jasper says, angry. "She's an adult now. She is free to make her own decisions."

My father waves his gun, motioning toward Brad. "Brad, you can leave now. Thank you for all of your hard work. Your father is waiting for you. He doesn't want you to get caught up in all of this, son. We will speak about this later."

Brad salutes my father and then hops off the back of the truck. He swirls his pointer finger in the air and cues his friends to pack everything up. "Time to head out," he says.

My father doesn't give him time to even climb into the passenger seat before dropping the next bomb. "The deal was made because your mother was having an affair with Thomas."

"What?" Brad and I say at the same time.

I hear the absolute heartbreak in Brad's voice, and I step out from behind Jasper. His grip tightens around me, and I look up at him, then lightly squeeze his side as he lets me go.

Brad shuts the door to his friend's truck and circles back around.

"Brad, leave," my father orders.

Brad's face is no longer excited but in complete shock. His lips are parted, and his eyebrows are narrowed, his jaw clenched. "No. I need to hear this, too. That's my father you are talking about."

"Fine, we're all adults, right?" my father slurs, laughing darkly. "They were having an affair. Eleanor figured it out while we were having dinner one night. She called them out on their bullshit, and they admitted to it. Your mother was going to leave me for him, Lillian! I couldn't believe it. My best friend and my wife!" He paces back and forth, waving the gun around. His chest rises and falls, anger boiling inside of him as all the memories flood back. He so desperately wants the memories to disappear, but the more he drinks, the more they surface. "I had to stop her, and Eleanor wanted nothing to do with any of the drama, so she shot your mother. She wanted to shoot Thomas too, but she wanted him to suffer a life without my wife. I'm not too keen on the details because he could have easily locked her up for what she did, but… She pays my bills and gives me everything that I want, so I'm not complaining. I just have to keep my mouth shut and do what she tells me to do now and again."

It feels as if a bus has hit me. A bus that is going over a hundred miles an hour. It doesn't even try to slow down, but speeds up and uses me as a speed bump. The air from my lungs is knocked loose, and I am suddenly suffocating. My hands tangle in my hair, and I pull slightly, my lips parting as I let out a desperate cry. My eyes burn from exhaustion, and the smoke lingers in the air, tears streaming down my face.

"Fuck!" Brad kicks a rock and grunts in frustration. He looks at me, hesitating. He wants to run to me and comfort me, but he doesn't. He lingers near before turning on his heel, getting into the truck and slamming the door behind him. He puts his hand on the outside of the door, hitting it twice to tell his friend he's ready to leave.

"I'm sorry, Lillian. I'm so sorry," he calls out the window, as they speed away from the scene.

The shop shifts and collapses. The fire gives off a heavy heat, and it no longer feels good in the cold night air. It's too hot and begins to sting my skin.

Jasper's hand finds mine, but he stays silent.

"Care to say what's on your mind, sweetheart?" My father sways. "I guess I finally found the right set of words to keep your mouth shut. You're not so tough now, are you?"

With every word he utters, I want to throw up.

"Enough," Jasper finally speaks. "Can't you see that you are hurting her?"

"I-I don't understand how you can be okay with this? You watched the woman you love die... right in front of you!" I scream through the tears. "What the hell is wrong with you? Do you even have a fucking soul?"

"No," he grins. "I sold my soul to the devil." His arm rises abruptly, aiming the gun at Jasper and firing.

My eyes widen as I feel Jasper's grasp loosen from my hand and then pull away altogether. A gasp leaves his lips, and I scream, turning and watching his body fall. It hits the ground with a large thud and his hand covering his chest. He attempts to sit up, but falls back and coughs.

I scrape my knees over the gravel as I fall down next to him. I move his head to my lap and hold pressure on his chest as the blood pours out of him and seeps through his clothing. "We have to get you to the hospital," my voice trembles. "You're going to be fine."

I look up to find my father gone. He left without a trace and without another word. He had one thing on his mind, and he had accomplished it for the night.

Jasper's blood is warm and thick as it oozes out. I strip his clothes away, seeing how bad the wound is, but only to learn that he was shot slightly to the side and more into his shoulder. "What shitty aim," Jasper tries to chuckle.

He grits his teeth and winces at the pain. I pull my phone out of my jacket pocket and begin to call for an ambulance. "What a shitty town. Ran by a fucking lunatic mayor—"

I hear sirens in the distance, throw my phone down, and focus on Jasper. His face is pale, his eyes heavy. He reaches up and cups my face, some blood smearing onto my cheek.

With a million different questions fighting for the forefront of my mind, the one question that comes to mind is, "Do you want me to call your mother?"

He nods and whispers the phone number to me. Tears form in his eyes, and with every blink, they fall. "I can't die, Lillian. I can't leave my son. He's already lost one parent," he sniffles. "He can't lose me, too."

I press the phone to my ear as the ambulance pulls down the driveway. Cops and fire trucks are not far behind. It makes me wonder who's in charge of this entire operation. The one who let time slip by while my father got away.

As the paramedics rush to his side and slide him onto the gurney, his hand reaches out for mine. I run to keep up, gripping his hand. I promise to stay by his side, trying to fight the tears and the thoughts that race in my mind.

They ask him questions, which he answers almost in a whisper. They are trying to keep him conscious by keeping him talking for as long as he can. I feel like I'm in a distant blur, watching. The rings from my phone grow quieter as the ambulance siren grows louder. It's cold and very bright within the vehicle, but the men are professional and amazing with Jasper.

The ringing stops. "Hello?"

"Erm, hi. My name is Lillian—"

She clears her throat. "I don't know what you are selling, but I'm not interested. Please take me off your calling list."

"No," I say, frustrated. I pinch the bridge of my nose and sigh. "I'm Jasper's fri... Listen, that's not even the point. Jasper's—" A sob escapes me.

"Hello? Jasper's what?"

What do I even tell this woman? The more I watch the paramedics work on Jasper, the more scared I become. I inhale a shaky breath. "Jasper's been shot. We are on our way to the hospital now. He asked if you would meet us there."

"Did you call Connor?"

"No." I shake my head. I bite on my nails and hunch over. My elbows are on my knees. I rocked back and forth as I watch Jasper pass out.

"He's losing a lot of blood," one paramedic says.

"His heart rate is declining," the other says.

His mother chokes out, "I'll call him and meet you there."

After major surgery and a few days, he is alive and on his way to recovery. I stay almost every day, frightened to leave his side. His mother spends most of her time with him in his room while I waited patiently for visiting hours in the waiting room with Connor. Every so often, she comes out and gives a report of his status and then quickly returns to his side for the rest of the night.

Other than frequent status updates, I haven't said two words to his mother. I suppose she blames me for everything that happened. I don't blame her. If I didn't have a dysfunctional life, he would be fine. Better, even.

One night, she comes looking for me and finds me puking in the bathroom stall, crying to myself. I had been running on adrenaline for the past few days, Jasper's dried blood all over me, and I'm finally crashing from exhaustion. She hugs me, and we sit there and cry together.

His son is nowhere to be seen. Connor says he's at his house, spending time with his mother and father. It excites Connor that his father came home from being on the road for the last few months, and he's also very grateful that he's there to help out with Jasper's son. It gives him time with his grandson, Connor says.

Within the next few days, Connor and I become acquainted with each other. He knows where my loyalty lies, and for that, he isn't as angry with me anymore. I think we find comfort within each other. We play card games and talk for hours on end. He trades me juicy stories about Jasper for snacks from the vending machine.

Of course, the cops are involved. I requested that I speak with an officer that wasn't at the crime scene that night. I don't trust any of them. After a good fight, they finally agree.

After the quick interview, the newspaper asks if I can come down to the station to do a report. I don't decline it, and frankly, I'm happy to if it means that my father is put behind bars and I never have to see him again. I stop by my house first to take a quick shower and pack some clothes since I know he won't be home. That's the first place they'd look for him.

The next morning, everything is suddenly on the front cover of our local newspaper. My father is found and arrested. His trial will be held in a few days, and I'm needed there to testify. Brad is also arrested. My father threw him under the bus the first chance he had and showed the cops every text message between them. It doesn't make a difference. The cops have figured it out anyway.

Now, it's time to take Jasper home. Jasper's mother wants nothing to do with any of our plans. She's assertive and wants her son home to rest, but Jasper has other plans.

"Just a quick detour," he begs from the backseat. His head is in the crook of my neck, his voice raspy. "I need to pick up my truck, and Lillian needs to get her bug."

"No," Anna argues. Her big brown eyes appear in the rearview mirror as she looks at him. "We are not going back there. I don't want to see it."

Jasper knows it'll bring his mother heartache to see the shop in a pile of ashes, but he wants his property somewhere safe, even if he can't drive for the time being. His mother tries to make up any excuse to not go to her late husband's old workplace, the very place they fell in love that became almost like a second home. Not only because Jasper's father owned it, but because they lived there for a few months before finding a home together. They had transformed the office into a tiny bedroom and ate out at the diner almost every night.

"Your father's old truck is at home. That should be good enough if you need to go anywhere."

"That's a classic, though," both Connor and Jasper chime in together.

"You don't want to drive that around town every day," Connor says from the front seat.

"I never did understand the love of an old car like your father did," his mother shakes her head. "It just sits there!"

"It's sexy as hell, though!" Connor nearly screams. The freckles on his face nearly jump off his nose out of excitement, until Anna slaps his arm out of annoyance.

"Fine!"

Jasper laughs quietly to himself, sighing as he watches the world roll by as we drive back to the shop in silence.

I think Jasper and I are both scared to go back. It's still freshly engraved within our skulls, a surreal experience that we experienced together, but we know eventually we'll have to face it together.

Without even a glance at the burned down shop, Anna pulls into the driveway and keeps her view down at her lap. She sucks her bottom lip in. Her cheeks flush as she holds her emotions inside.

Once we are out of the vehicle, with Connor tagging along, she speeds away. I'd like to think she had at least one look at the place and is now grateful no one is with her so she can grieve alone and have time to breathe from the past few days of thinking her son was going to die.

Connor suggests that he'll drive Jasper home and that I can follow, but Jasper won't have it. He isn't harsh, but he explains that he doesn't want to be away from me, that the hospital was torture enough, and with the trauma that we both went through, we're a done deal at this point.

With Jasper's help, I drive his truck home. I admit it's pretty scary driving a ten-ton monster, but I like being high off the ground.

"He just doesn't understand," Jasper says, talking about Connor. "No one will."

I don't want to think about that night. I don't want to think about my father and his little secret that only the

Taylors seem to know about. I have so many questions based on that whole situation, but I think it's best to not ask. It will be opening Pandora's box and a lifetime of hurt. More damage than what's already done.

"He won't, but he wasn't mad, either, Jas. He looked like he understood." I shrug. My eyes don't leave the road, and the wheel is basically in my lap. I pull the seat forward and straighten my back. I don't understand how he drives so laid back, but I don't have his long legs, either. "I like Connor."

I see Jasper smile, and his hand suddenly touches my leg. "Y'all got to have an actual civil conversation at the hospital, didn't you?"

I nod. "Even though I wanted you because I feel like nothing will repair our pain like each other's company, I had him when visiting hours were over and I couldn't be with you. We just traded stories and learned about each other."

"Well, darlin', if you're sticking around, it needs to happen. I'm glad it happened naturally and not forced. Connor is a big part of my life, and just like my son, he is also part of my package."

I gulp, nervous. This will be the first time I'm meeting his son, and I didn't even put two thoughts into it. I've been so preoccupied with everything else.

"I'm not going anywhere." I shake my head. I quickly grab his hand and glance in his direction. "You took a fucking bullet for me, Jasper. Who the hell does that? You haven't even known me for four months, and you took a fucking bullet for me."

He chuckles, his thumb rubbing the back of my palm. "You sound like I had a choice," he jokes.

"Well," I giggle. "That's fair... But you don't hear about those types of things unless you love the person. I just think—"

"Maybe I do love you, Lillian Grace Abernathy."

I nearly choke on my saliva as the words pour out of his mouth as he whispers into my ear. I thought I was imagining things. Only hearing what I wanted to hear. "You love me?" I almost want to cry. It's been so long since I've heard anyone say those words.

"I took a fucking bullet for you," he mocks. "Yeah, I'd say I love you. I don't see myself going anywhere anytime soon. I just see you and me. If you'll have me?"

"Jasper James Smith, you idiot. Of course I'll have you."

I have never been on a more emotional rollercoaster.

My hands feel clammy as they wrap around the steering wheel, holding on for dear life. My stomach launches into my throat as my rear end leaves the safety of my seat, jumping slightly into the air as we drive over numerous bumps and potholes.

"Almost there, I promise," he reassures me. His hand slides onto my knee as his eyes study the road. He groans after every pothole we hit. "Try to go easy, please?"

After a moment of silence, the bumps disappear, and we reach a paved road that winds up a small hill. A small blue trailer sits on top of it. They attached a new cedar porch to the front of it, and his father's red truck sits in the driveway. My yellow beetle sits off to the side with Connor behind the wheel, patiently waiting, Anna's Honda Civic parked next to it.

"You really live out in the middle of nowhere," my voice trails off, as we pull beside the red truck, my view toward the backyard, a wide-open field like the one behind his mechanic shop. Just endless mountains and hills. Clouds leave shadows dancing across the hills as the sky becomes shifts and becomes clear.

"You act surprised."

"Well, I guess not. Just observing."

"I like peace, Lillian."

"Our small town doesn't already offer that enough?"

He leans closer to me and turns the truck off, the keys dangling in the ignition. He falls back into his seat, wincing from the pain. They wrapped his shoulder and chest up underneath his red and black checkerboard shirt. He looks at me, almost disappointed, and it makes my skin crawl.

"Sadly, no. You said it yourself, the whole town is so far up everyone's asses. Everyone knows each other's names. If not, they sure know your cousin."

I laugh.

"Lillian, I want to go where no one knows my name or my story. I don't want to go to a fancy big town or anything like that, but somewhere barren. Where it takes nearly an hour to go into town and where the neighbors are miles apart."

Alone. That is what he craves to be. The town paints a picture of him from his past mistakes and the loss he had to grieve through. Instead of asking, they assumed. I understand that, especially after everything that has happened. That's all I've wanted to be—alone.

"That sounds almost like a dream," I breathe. The thought of it sinks in. "I wouldn't care to be alone, either. I never have time to just think. To consume the world around me."

"I wouldn't say completely alone. I'd build my mama her own house, not too far away, so she can still see Grayson and my other future children."

"Future children, huh?"

"I'd be married, of course."

I grin. "Is that so?"

He chuckles. "Do you honestly think that I would just stay single for the rest of my life?"

My cheeks flush. "Well, no. I just… It surprises me that you have a plan for your life."

"I have to. Being a father, I can't just dwell on tomorrow. I have to have a plan, and I want to do better for my child. It might take time to get there, but I have a plan… Don't you? Have you ever thought about your future?"

"Uh, I honestly haven't thought about it too much. My goal was to leave after I graduate, but then I met you. Then, you kind of fucked up my plans."

"Sorry," he grins. "You don't think about getting married? Having kids? Doing your dream job and whatever hobbies that make you happy?"

"Nope, not really. My whole life I have had that Disney dream. Where I would find the love of my life for the first time, have kids, grow old and die. Before my mother died, I wanted to be a chef or something in that realm, but I don't know now. Everything has changed. I have changed."

"What about hobbies? What do you like to do for fun?"

I think for a second, but I can't remember the last time I've done something for myself, besides standing up to Brad and my father. "I don't have any," I finally say.

He narrows his eyes at me. "Everyone has hobbies."

"Nope, not me."

"Well, what do you do when you're alone in bed?"

My jaw slightly drops. "Jasper Smith, we just officially became a couple, and you are already asking me the dirtiest of questions!" My tone is smooth like butter, and for a moment, I hope he knows I'm kidding. I smirk, adding to the flirting. "What do you do for fun?"

"I like to read."

I cock my head to the side, and my eyes grow wide. "You don't strike me as someone who likes to read."

He shrugs. "What am I supposed to like? Hunting? Fishing? All of that manly stuff that everyone else around this small town likes to do?" He leans over and reaches below his seat, pulling out an almost decrepit book. The spine has weakened, and he struggles to hold the pages inside. He hands it over and lays it on my lap, leaning against the door of the vehicle, and grabs his chest, gritting his teeth in pain. After a second of realizing that I'm staring at him, making sure he is okay, he motions me to look at the book.

Gone With the Wind, the cover reads. By Margaret Mitchell.

"Romance?" I lightly giggle. "You just continue to amaze me."

He leans over and points at the cover. "One of the best romance novels ever written. It's not just about romance but has some manly parts in it. It talks about the war and the great state of Georgia... I'm a history nerd, too."

I shake my head, grinning like a fool. To hear about his wants and his needs, his likes and dislikes... To hear about the way of his life and what makes his heart tickle. It makes me happy, makes me want to listen. It makes me want more.

His bright eyes shoot up at me, a dimple forming in the corner of his cheek. "What?" he asks, lowering his voice.

"You're not real. Someone's fairytale. You are a man that just simply doesn't exist." My voice trails off, and my words grow quiet.

His eyes search mine, and he grabs my face, pulling me toward him until our lips clash.

My eyes shut, and I melt away in the moment. This is the same feeling I had when Brad allowed me to be alone for the first time in ages. The freedom. The butterflies rock my heart against my chest. This moment has a feeling that nothing in this world could destroy. Happiness. Bliss. Time feels endless.

His soft lips move, and it's no longer just a lingering peck, but something a little more, our lips dancing. He slightly pulls away, and his forehead falls against mine, his chest rising and falling. "Darlin', you are bad news."

Before I can answer him with a smart remark, Connor is at his window, knocking. A smug look is on his freckled face, and his blue eyes are a pale glow. He shifts his jaw out of embarrassment.

"I hate to break up this lover sesh, but I hear your son getting rowdy inside. I think he's getting impatient with waiting."

For the last few years, I've made it my mission to not care. When it came to meeting someone's family, I didn't care how I presented myself. I didn't want to make an impression. I figured that I would never see them again anyway, so why kiss ass? But this is different. I want to make an impression. A good one. And honestly? It scares the hell out of me.

Especially being that special family member is my significant other's child. Children are so bluntly honest, and you don't want to spoil them to get them to like you, but then again, you want to show you care. I don't have any experience with children, but I hope this is the first of many good experiences with this one.

We both get out of the truck and make our way up the paved walkway, leading up to the porch stairs. My converse hit the edge of the step as I began to hear his son scream from inside. The nerves finally set in, and I attempt to unravel the knots forming in my stomach.

Jasper and Connor have already made it to the front door, the screen door swinging open as the little boy runs into his father's arms. Jasper's lengthy body rocks on his heels as Greyson nearly knocks him over. He scoops the child up, hugging him tightly as Greyson lays his head on his father's shoulder, Jasper wincing with a smile. The boy has some similar features to his father, but he looks just like his mother. Freckles lay across his button nose. His eyes are brown, and his eyebrows are thick. His dark hair is cut into a bowl shape around his head.

"Careful," Connor reminds him. "Don't be too tough on your daddy."

Jasper doesn't acknowledge Connor's comment. He's too busy eyeing his child's head. "Who the hell cut his hair?" Jasper nearly yells, looking into the house.

"He needed a haircut, Jasper. Poor thing could barely see," Anna's voice grows louder, as she gets closer to the door. "I asked Connor's mother to cut it for him while we were at the hospital."

Jasper sets Greyson down, his hand reaching underneath his chin and raising it to get a better look. "I told you I was going to take him to the barber shop sometime this week," his voice growls out of annoyance.

"Oh, I forgot."

Jasper sighs, shaking his head and looking at his son. "You look nice," he compliments. "What made you get all dressed up?"

"I wanted to look nice for your coming home party," Greyson grins. "What was it like getting shot?"

The air falls silent. Jasper is slightly in shock and struggles for words. "Son, hopefully, you will never have to find out what it's like. It hurts like hell."

"So, like stepping on a Lego?"

Everyone begins to laugh. It's nice to kind of laugh about the situation, but it's tough talking about it. And it reminds me that Jasper and I have court in a few days for it.

Connor bends down and picks at the little boy's denim long-sleeve button-up. "You missed a button, little dude. Want me to fix it?"

Greyson's face wrinkles and turns sour. "No, I got it. I did it all by myself. I can fix it all on my own, too."

The boy begins to unbutton his shirt but quickly stops as his eyes find me. He quickly turns toward Jasper and points to me. "Who is that?"

I've been so focused on observing that I forgot to climb the stairs to introduce myself.

Anna peeks outside, her long hair flowing in the wind as her dark eyes gaze at me. "Jasper," she says. "Why is that pretty young lady standing at the edge of our porch? Where are your manners? Invite Lillian in."

"Is she here with Connor?" Greyson adds.

My heart nearly sinks, and I begin to question my motives. I don't want to add confusion to his son's life, especially since we haven't informed people what we were labeling our relationship, even though it's probably pretty clear by this point.

"Uh, no. Greyson, this is Lillian Abernathy." He motions me closer. "She's a very good friend of mine. She's come to welcome me home."

I can't make my feet move, and I find myself stuck.

Connor smirks. "For once, she's silent. Interesting."

What if he doesn't like me? What if I'll never be good enough for him? I know I'll never be good enough.

I find my footing and slowly make my way up the stairs, a hand tightly gripping my purse strap. My thumb rubs against the leather.

Who am I right now? The woman I have created is slowly washing away, and I reveal a weakling.

"Hi," I squeak. "It's good to finally meet you. I've heard so many things about you."

His dark caramel eyes squint at me. "Oh yeah? What did Daddy tell you?"

"Well," I begin. I look up at Anna as she stands in the doorway and holds the screen door open. She gives an encouraging smile and waits. I look back down. "He said that you are into bugs, that you must know thousands of different types, and you love to eat chili, and you like to watch old western movies."

His snarl relaxes as he grins. Dimples sink into his cheeks, and for a moment, I see a glimpse of his father. "I like her," he says, turning to look at Jasper. "She can stay."

Now

Connor

Her face is pale. The information is sinking in, and parts of her mind are trying to connect. She squints slightly and turns to Brad. "What happened? Did y'all face any real jail time?"

Brad clears his throat and shifts uncomfortably on the tiny stool. "I spent a year in prison. My parents paid a fine, and they also paid Jasper for all the damages. I'm in therapy and taking anger management classes as well." He sounds almost proud of himself, but the look on her face screams *not impressed*. She knows he should have faced more consequences.

In her mind, I guess, they finally broke through to some sort of friendship level or whatever is between stranger and friend, I, personally, want nothing to do with him.

"Your father, on the other hand," he begins. "They released him from prison a month ago. He has been in prison for the past two years and has to finish his time on parole. They force him to go to AA meetings and to anger management. Occasionally, he goes to therapy as well."

She scoffs, rolling her eyes. Her arms are tightly crossed against her chest. "Obviously, he hasn't learned a single fucking lesson," she says. "He's still the same man, trying to manipulate me into becoming the same person I was two years ago so he can try to get money out of your parents."

Brad shakes his head, handing it for a second and rubbing the palm of his hands together. "Yeah, I don't understand it, either. They don't want him around anymore. He tried to snitch on them for what happened to your mother, hoping that it would relieve his sentence."

Her blue eyes grow wide, and she sits up, her arms dropping to her sides. She grips her sheets tightly. "Did it work?"

"No," he admits. "They didn't believe him. That and I think my parents have some kind of ties on the inside."

She sighs. "I wouldn't be surprised."

It's hard to comprehend what is going on inside Lillian's mind. I'm sure everything is still fresh and very emotional to hear. She cries silently and stares down at her white cotton sheets.

Her cheeks turn a shade of pink, and her glistening eyes finally turn to me. "I'm sorry," she says, almost in a whisper. She laughs slightly and begins to frantically wipes the tears away from her face.

"It's okay," I say and reach for her hand.

"It's a lot," Brad adds. "We've had two years to digest this information. You've not even had a week."

She nods. Her eyes search the room for a moment, and you can tell she's in deep thought as questions pop up in her mind. She takes a deep breath and then asks, "What about Jasper? What happened after our court date? Did he buy another mechanic shop?"

I find it slightly amusing to rub their relationship in Brad's face. Deep down, I hope he realizes what he lost and what he could have had if he had just acted right. "Uh. No, he didn't. He used the money the Taylors gave him to get you out of Georgia and away from any more conflict."

"Really?" She smiles.

I rub her hand softly. "We moved to Tennessee. We bought some property and built three houses on it. They aren't the biggest houses, but it was an upgrade from our trailers. One for your tiny family, one for his mother, and one for me."

"And you said I was going to become a stepmother?"

I nod. "Jasper was going to ask you to marry him the day we got into the car accident. We were on our way to some cliff-side up in the mountains. He spent weeks trying to find the perfect place to propose."

She blinks, the smile fading away from her lips. "How does our story end, Connor?"

I scoot my chair closer and smile. "It doesn't... it hasn't. Not if you don't want it to."

Lillian sighs. She quickly turns to Brad and asks him to go to the nurses' station so she can take her father off the visitation list. She no longer wants to see him.

Once the door closes behind Brad, she retracts her hand from me. "In my mind, the story never happened. None of it... When I see Jasper, I see a stranger."

The words are like daggers to my heart and a punch to my gut. I rise to my feet, gripping my hair. "Lillian, just give it time. He-he is going to wake up... an-and things are going to go back to normal," I stutter, as I try to find the words. My mind is all over the place.

"Things will be normal to him, but not to me. That's not fair. To him or me."

"Lillian, there is no Jasper without you."

"What am I supposed to do? Play pretend?" Her voice cracks.

I realize that I'm only upsetting her for selfish reasons. How am I supposed to explain this to Jasper?

She cocks her head to the side, grabbing my hand. "You tried your best to help me regain my memory, and for that, I'm so grateful. Do you hear me? I'm so fucking grateful that you never lied to me. That you told me every bit of truth that everyone tried to hide from me despite how I felt about it in the end. You are a genuine friend, Connor. I can't thank you enough for what you have done," she says calmly.

I bite my lip and sit down abruptly. "That's it then?"

"Connor…"

"Please." I put my hands together in a praying motion. "I'm begging you to think about this. The information has been a lot on you, and you aren't thinking clearly. I think you haven't had time to think at all, let alone process anything from the past week. Please. Just sleep on it?"

She shakes her head. "Fine. I suppose you're right."

It wasn't long after that I left, leaving the notebook behind. That is her story. Of course, I didn't write down everything, telling her half of it from experience, but I hope it's enough for her to get her gears moving.

On the way out, I find Brad and her father arguing in the hospital parking lot. Her father refuses to believe that his daughter doesn't want anything to do with him. He begins to grow frustrated and angry, punching his vehicle. "This is your fault," he screams at me. "You bastard! I'll kill you for this!"

I ignore him, smiling to myself as I feel a sense of accomplishment.

❀ ❀ ❀

The next morning, I find Lillian gathering up her things and packing her bag. She's in an oversized hoodie and a pair of leggings, her hair up in a messy bun. Her eyes are tired, and black rings circle them.

I want to ask if she got any sleep, but my gut knows otherwise. She actually considered my offer. She probably read the story again, but this time all alone with no one's input.

She smiles at me and shoves the notebook into her suitcase. "I hope you don't mind," she whispers. "It's comforting, in a way."

I lean my shoulder against the doorframe and shake my head, waving my hand around. "No, go ahead. I'm glad you enjoyed it."

Silence fills the room.

I'm so eager to know her thoughts, but I can't bear to ask.

She turns to her nightstand and throws a yellow envelope toward me, flying through the air until it lands at the end of the bed. She rubs her lower back with the palms of her hands anxiously.

She doesn't have to say a thing, though. I can already tell what she's thinking.

Disappointment sinks in as I shove the lump in my throat down. I lean forward and snatch the envelope from the bed.

Jasper.

I shake my head, closing my eyes tightly as my eyes burn. My face feels flushed, and I let out a deep sigh as I cry.

"Please give that to him. If he wakes up," she says.

"Yup."

"I'm sure in another life, or multiverse, we could have worked. But in this timeline, it was obvious that God had other plans. We weren't destined to be together."

"Where will you go?" My voice comes out stronger than I intend it to.

She zips her suitcase up and then tucks a strand of ginger hair behind her ear. It scares her to make eye contact. "I, uh... Brad gave me some cash to get myself a hotel room. Just until I figure out what I want to do with my life."

"That's nice of him." I roll my eyes.

"Don't be like that."

"Well, how do you want me to be?"

"Happy for me? That I'm no longer a prisoner in my own life. Thanks to you."

It's hard being happy when I want to be selfish. I don't want her to leave. I'm losing a best friend, but in a way, I know she's right. I don't want her to be right.

195

I shake my head, grinning. "This would have gone so much better if Jasper was awake. I swear just the sound of his voice would have knocked that memory back into place."

She laughs. "Yeah, probably. Thank you for trying, though. It is a beautiful story, but it's just not mine."

"No, Lillian. It's yours. And when the time comes, it will live on."

Without hesitation, she leaps into my arms and hugs me tightly around the neck. Her face nestles into my neck, and I can feel her face damp with tears. "I hope one day I love someone as much as he loved me," she whispers.

It took letting her go to realize that I was holding on to nothing. That in the end it meant nothing to her anyway. It was just a story, but to me, it was so much more, and she will never realize that.

These last few days have been so bittersweet to me. I got to spend some of the last moments with my best friend, telling her a story about her life and the type of woman she turned out to be, and it just so happens to be the woman she always hoped she would turn into.

But now... she's finally free.

Epilogue

Connor

It has been one week since I last saw Lillian. It hurts to think about how she just walked out of our lives, but after thinking about it for a week, I know I was wrong. She deserves to live her life the way she wants to live it, even if that means me not being a part of it.

Jasper has woken up. The doctor has been asking him questions for the past hour, making sure he didn't lose any memory, too. So far, he hasn't. He gets information mixed up, but other than that, he's okay.

Once the doctor leaves, it's just us. Anna left the hospital to grab a shower and pick up Greyson from my parents' house.

"Why hasn't anyone mentioned Lillian? How is she?" he asks, his voice raspy. His throat will be sore for a while from the breathing tube. His dark hair is a mess, and nearly all of his cuts are healed. His pale face is slowly showing shades of color.

I wipe the sweat off my palms on the back of my pants and sit down. "I-I, erm… She's good," I choke. My guts knot inside my stomach, and I'm in desperate need of a bucket. "She was in a coma, too. She's awake, though, and they discharged her a week ago."

His face falls. "Oh, that's insane. Where is she now? Is she with Greyson or something? I don't understand why she isn't here…"

I shift uncomfortably in my chair. "Jasper, there's something I have to tell you."

"What? Where is she, Connor?" His voice is scared. "Where is she?"

Instead of answering any more questions for him, I lean to the side and pull the yellow envelope from my back pocket. I slide it onto the bed next to his hand, gulping as tears pile up in the corner of my eyes.

His jaw clenches as he grabs the envelope, ripping through the yellow paper. He unfolds the letter and reads it. Once he is done, he throws the letter onto the floor and stares up at the ceiling. "She lost her memory," he whispers. "She lost her fucking memory!" He cries, kicking the blanket off his legs abruptly. "I have to leave this damn hospital. I have to find her." He pulls the IV out of his arm and sits up. "She has to remember me."

I scramble to my feet and grab his shoulders, pushing him back down onto the bed. His face is flushed, and his blue eyes are wide, tears streaming down his face. His lower lip quivers. "Get the fuck off me, Connor." His hands try to rip my arms off him. He grunts and huffs.

"Stop!" I scream. "Don't be stupid, Jasper."

"How can you say that?" he screams back. He's now in my face, and I can hear his heartbreak with every single word. "She is the love of my life, and you're just going to tell me to let her go?"

"Yes," I say calmly, as I sit on the edge of the bed. He sinks back down into the pillows as I drop my arms to my side. I avoid looking at his arm, blood drizzling out from where he had pulled his IV out. "I told her everything she needed to know. She has the damn journal I wrote her. She just needs time."

"Time," he scoffs.

"Listen," I snap. "I know it's hard for you to understand, but she didn't want to be a burden to you. She didn't want to be trapped in another life that she knew nothing about. Just give her some time, and maybe she will come back around."

"Do you think so?"

"Jasper, you're the only one who holds the right answers. She'll find her way back to you. She has to."

As he wipes his eyes with the palms of his hands, he nods aggressively. "Okay," he agrees. He thinks for a moment. "Thank you for being there for her when I couldn't. That means a lot to me. You've always been such a great brother to me. You could have drifted away after Sky died, but you didn't."

I grab his hand and shake my head. "I couldn't leave you. Like now, we needed each other back then to lean on and patch away the pain."

Just as our bonding moment blossoms, my nephew runs into the room. He screams and jumps onto the bed, crawling up to his dad and hugging his neck tightly. "I missed you," Greyson whispers. "You scared me."

"I missed you, too, bud. I'm so sorry. It's okay now. I promise."

Thank you for reading!
Please add a review on Amazon and let me know what you thought!

Amazon reviews are extremely helpful for authors, thank you for taking the time to support me and my work. Don't forget to share your review on social media with the hashtag #HoldingOntoNothing and encourage others to read the story too!!

Acknowledgements

Where do I even begin? My heart is so full of love for so many people. I couldn't have done this without so many of you pushing me to pursue my dream.

First, I want to say thank you to the Moms Who Write group. You guys have been there from the start and are the sweetest group of women; you are so supportive and have pushed me every step of the way.

My beta readers are next, of course. Thank you to Jasmine Harris, Ashlyn Delill, Kristina Bosch, Katie Stauffer, Judith Carre, Jenna Emm, Rebecca Leanne Villa, Brittany Purrtteman, and Shelby Knapp. Without you all believing in me and helping me bring my story to life, I wouldn't have the courage to put myself out there. Thank you for falling in love with my writing.

Whitney Morsillo for shaping my vision and pushing me further into my journey.

GetCover for the amazing cover art. I didn't have a vision for it, but I put all my trust into your creative minds. You truly brought my book to life.

My mother and my mother-in-law, you have supported me and have loved me every step of the way.

To Mark, my darling husband and the father to our beautiful child, whom I have loved since I was fourteen. You get your hands dirty, so I can keep mine clean. You have given me the time to make my dreams a reality and so I can raise our child to be the very best she can be. You mean so much to me.

Thank you all for being in my life and for supporting me.

Don't forget to sign up for the newsletter!

For special offers, giveaways, discounts, bonus content, updates from the author, information on new releases and other great reads, visit:
https://www.savannahschmidtbooks.com

Savannah Schmidt is a debut romance author spending her days in North Georgia with her daughter and husband. With a degree in Media and Communications, she actually began her creative journey in elementary school, writing chapter books about animals and comics about her grandmother's cat, and she believes that there's always "a story that hasn't been told yet." When she isn't writing fiercely independent heroines finding their unique voice, she likes to play video games and take her young daughter on Starbucks dates, shopping Ingles and sharing a pink drink.

Connect With Savannah On:
Website:
https://www.savannahschmidtbooks.com
Facebook:
https://www.facebook.com/profile.php?id=100090107542769

CPSIA information can be obtained
at www.ICGtesting.com
Printed in the USA
BVHW070146290423
663281BV00010B/285